Fred Wander was born in Vienna in [ ] Buchenwald and several other conc[ ] moved to the GDR to study at the Literature Institute in Leipzig, returning to Vienna in 1980. He received the Theodor Kramer Prize in 2003. Fred Wander died in 2006.

Michael Hofmann is the highly acclaimed translator of Joseph Roth, Wolfgang Koeppen, Kafka and Brecht and the author of several books of poems and a book of criticism. He lives in London and Hamburg.

'This is a wonderful, terrible and inspiring book . . . It deserves to be placed alongside classics of survival such as Julius Fucik's *Report from the Gallows* and Primo Levi's *If This Is a Man' Morning Star*

'Books, as Levi reminds us, have their own fates. Wander's, written twenty-five years after the events it describes, has had a long, hard journey into our hands, but, with the help of Michael Hofmann's excellent translation, we are at last in possession of a masterpiece to rank alongside those of Primo Levi and Imre Kertesz' *Jewish Quarterly Review*

'A collection of concise and haunting anecdotes . . . [this is a] distressing, yet beautifully written book.' *New Statesman*

'In a superb new translation by Michael Hofmann, Wander does not guide the reader on his own journey from boxcar to barbed wire, as Elie Wiesel and Primo Levi have done. Rather, his anonymous narrator undergoes a sort of spiritual education as he studies the doomed men and boys around him. The result is an indirect portrait of a man trying to grasp an unthinkable trauma' *New York Times*

'Complete and affecting . . . it contributes something new to this canon: bonhomie . . . This is a Holocaust novel that celebrates European Jewry as much as it laments its fate' *New York Sun*

'Michael Hofmann's exquisite translation, acutely attuned to the multiculturalism of the camps, subtly indicates both the cacophony of languages heard . . . and the mood of companionship.' *TLS*

'Some novels are imagined, others are lived. The slim but immensely powerful *The Seventh Well* is the latter . . . [Wander] will be remembered for his remarkable understanding of the largeness of life' *San Francisco Chronicle*

'In Wander's book we have the testament of a true survivor, honest, non-judgemental, devoid of self-pity. Someone able to integrate the horror of the camps with the richer world beyond, which each character brings with him in some form. This is a necessary book so that we may, in the words of Rabbi Lowe of Prague, emerge from the darkness with clear eyes and free hearts' Eva Figes

'Comparisons to both classic concentration-camp memoirs and Alexander Solzhenitsyn's *One Day in the Life of Ivan Denisovich* are as justly earned as they are inevitable . . . A story we cannot hear too many times is grippingly retold in this blistering report from hell on earth. Wander's legacy thus becomes a gift bequeathed to all of us' *Kirkus Reports*

'Among the most significant chroniclers of the Dark Age of the Holocaust, Elie Wiesel is the prophet, Primo Levi the scientist, Paul Celan the poet. And now, in *The Seventh Well,* here is Fred Wander, yet another voice risen out of the ashes, who embodies what we might call the Adversarial Conscience of that merciless night. Though he shows us, as he ineluctably must, the bloodthirsty nature of the atrocities and their perpetrators, he is even more intent on illuminating the "stainless transparency" of the violated. Here you will meet humanely civilized souls who are named and known and felt; and you cannot come away from this account and still declare yourself egalitarian' Cynthia Ozick

'[Wander] portrays . . . the strong and the weak, the rebellious and the passive, the pious and the unbelieving, the proud and the humble, the young and the old, Jews from all of Europe . . . in his unique and personal attempt to confront the most important experience of all' Christa Wolf

'In a harrowing, intensely moving narrative, Wander gives back to lost people their voices. Shockingly brutal, profoundly transcendent' *Seattle Times*

THE
SEVENTH
WELL

FRED WANDER

*Translated from the German
by Michael Hofmann*

GRANTA

Granta Publications, 12 Addison Avenue, London W11 4QR

First published in Great Britain by Granta Books 2008
This paperback edition published by Granta Books 2009
Published by arrangement with W.W. Norton & Company, Inc.

This translation was supported by the
Austrian Federal Ministry of Education, Arts and Culture.

Originally published in German as *Der Siebente Brunnen*

A CIP catalogue record for this book
is available from the British Library.

1 3 5 7 9 10 8 6 4 2

ISBN 978 1 84708 067 7

Printed in the UK by CPI Bookmarque, Croydon, CR0 4TD

In memory of my daughter

KITTY

CONTENTS

The seventh well—water of honesty,

Cleansed of all impurities;

Proof against defilement;

Of stainless transparency;

Prepared for future peoples,

That they may emerge from the darkness,

With clear eyes and free hearts.

from "The Seven Garlanded Wells"
by Rabbi Loew of Prague, died 1609

Fred Wander,
Europe 1938–1945

EAST
PRUSSIA   Sobibór

RUSSIA

GERMANY   Gross-Rosen
rschberg   Beuthen (Bytom)

Auschwitz

Riesengebirge
Mountains

Vienna

Salzburg

HUNGARY

RUMANIA

YUGOSLAVIA

BULGARIA

CHRONOLOGY

FRED WANDER, MAY 1938–JUNE 1945

The Seventh Well is a work of fiction inspired by many of the experiences of Fred Wander during the following years.

Emigration after the invasion of the Nazis in Austria (May 1938–September 1939)

1938

Beginning of May	Fred Wander flees Vienna via Nauders in Tirol at the border of Switzerland, Austria, and Italy.
Mid-May	Continues through Annecy to Lyon in southern France.
End of May	Arrives in Paris, where he is registered with the authorities until September 1939.

1939

First half of the year	Wander keeps moving; he travels from Paris to Avignon, Montpellier, Toulouse, Nantes, Saint-Nazaire, and Le Havre.
August/September	Returns to Paris, where he lives on rue Saint-André des Arts.

Internment in September 1939, the beginning of the war

September	Detained at Stade de Colombes, a temporary camp six miles west of Paris.
September 19	Transferred to a permanent internment camp in Meslay-du-Maine through January 26, 1940.

1940

January 26 through early June	Whereabouts unknown.
Beginning of June	Appears in camps at Angouleme, Perigueux (Dordogne), and Toulouse. Makes multiple escapes.
Summer	Captured south of Tarbes at the foot of Pic du Midi-de-Bigorre. Wander is released, makes his way back to Toulouse.
Autumn	Harvests grapes in Toulouse. Flees in the direction of Marseille but is captured en route.
November	Brought to Camp Saint-Antoine (Albi-Tarn).

1941–1942

	Wander flees and is recaptured several times, imprisoned in several work camps in southern France—Gurs, Le Vernet, Les Milles, Saint Cyprien, Argeles-sur-mer, and Lager Agde.
June through September 1941	Appears in camps at Montpellier, Lager Sete, and Abbaye de Valmagne.
Until summer 1942	Flight to Marseille. He is recaptured and returned to camp.

1942

August	Attempts to escape once more, heads to Switzerland. He is captured by the Vichy police, then deported to another holding camp.
End of August / beginning of September	Arrives at the internment camp in Rivesaltes.
September 12–16	Held briefly in Drancy.
September 16	Deported from Drancy to Auschwitz, concentration camp in Poland.

Concentration camps, from September 1942
through April 1945

September 1942 through May 1943	Wander is forced to work at several satellite camps of Auschwitz near Beuthen.

1943

May	Death march to Gross-Rosen. Transported to several satellite camps of Gross-Rosen, forced to perform slave labor breaking rocks and building streets for IG Farben and its Buna (rubber) factory. At the time, IG Farben was one of the biggest German chemical companies. It was dissolved after the war due to its strong Nazi ties.
Until winter 1944/1945	Gross-Rosen. Death march to Hirschberg and over the Riesengebirge ("Giant Mountains").

1945

January	Transferred to Buchenwald, a concentration camp in Germany.
February through March	Constructs underground shelters while imprisoned at Crawinkel/Ohrdruf, a satellite camp of Buchenwald near Arnstadt.
March	Death march back to Buchenwald.
April 11	Wander is officially liberated by the U.S. Army. His freedom is delayed, however, as he comes down with tuberculosis and spotted fever and must remain in the infirmary at the camp.
June	Return via Salzburg to Vienna in order to find his family. Wander discovers that all except his brother have been murdered in Auschwitz or Sobibór.

THE
SEVENTH
WELL

1

HOW TO
TELL A STORY

In the beginning was a conversation. Three weeks after the conversation, Mendel died. I didn't know he was going to die, nor of course did Mendel himself. He was already very weak, but still intensely engaged with everything around him. Wherever we were, on the march, or in the timber yard unloading tree trunks, he would deluge us with expressions of bitter contempt, evocations of beauty, dark poetical prophesyings, his word-torrent, his pride. I remember the time when one of the guards emptied a bucket of water over him. (Out of tiredness and weakness, Mendel had fallen asleep on his feet when he was supposed to be stacking wood.) The jackboots all fell about laughing (it was freezing cold that day, they were all bundled up in sheepskins, had cheeks flushed with warmth and big meals). Meanwhile Mendel drew himself up to his full height, his wet gray hair smeared over his brow, and his eyes peered out sharply, not with hate or accusation, but with curiosity. What is driving this man, those eyes wanted to know.

Every other Sunday afternoon (we had just two rest days a month) Mendel would tell stories. Everyone collected in the mess hall. Jews from Warsaw, from Sosnowiec and Krakow, all fascinated by the word. Words had magical powers, they could conjure up an entire beautiful lost world—a richly laid Sabbath table, the winsome loveliness of a Jewish girl, the heady aroma of sweet Palestine wine and raisin cake. It could take just one word to make the men turn pale, make them think, cry, laugh; words lashed them, choked them, made them ache and sweat. And all the time the master of words, the magician, Mendel Teichmann, perhaps fifty years old, tall, gaunt, and burning with an inner flame, stood before them on a bench, talking and waving his arms.

When he took me aside that time to talk to me (they were celebrating Passover just then, hiding in the wash-house, but he, who would have been the high priest of their dreams, happened not to believe in God), we scurried past the barracks so as not to draw the guards' attention, the twenty or so barracks in the Hirschberg camp in the Giant Mountains. Trembling, I blurted out that I would like to learn the art of the storyteller from him. I thought at first he had ignored or overheard my remark, but then he surprised me with a spate of words whose import I would only understand much later. But how am I to reproduce it—in comparison with the force and the splendor of his talk, my report is merely stammering.

"So you want to know how to tell a story? Well," Mendel said, "either you have it in you or you don't. Once, I think it was in Lodz or Warsaw, I had been among friends, telling stories on the Sabbath, and a whey-faced boy came up to me. 'Huh,' he said in embarrassment, the young whippersnapper, but with reproach in his eyes, 'it's one thing if a person's been around the way you have. But what have I got to tell stories about? I wouldn't mind being a writer like you, but I've had no experience!'

" 'I like it when people say that to me,' I answer, and I start asking the young man questions. How can such a thing be, I ask, and where did he live, because so far as I knew there wasn't anywhere in the world where you could hide from life. He lived in an old house, on an evil-smelling street on the edge of a town. He'd lived there from the day he was born, and it was all he knew. A house full of stupid, loathsome people. It could make you sick, the mere sight of them . . . He didn't say much more, my aspiring young man, but it was enough for me—I can see the house before me, I can smell it. I don't even need to go there to look at it.

"The second you walk in, a door opens, and a nosy old man peeps out at you. He's newly shaved, and there are traces of soap still on his cheeks. His braces are hanging off him, and while he finishes buttoning his patched shirt, you get a glimpse of his white scrawny body, the bones and sinews prominent the way they are in people who have worked all their lives. So he sticks his head out the door, and he asks me who I'm looking for, or if I'm lost. Because God knows how rarely a stranger happens by. I say the name of the young man, but the old man shakes his head, no, not known here. Then suddenly, as if he's just remembered, he changes his mind. Oh yes, the little devil upstairs, of course, I had the wrong name for him, his real name was Mottl Leiser but he was sure I meant him, I couldn't mean anyone else. Mottl terrorized the whole house, the house trembled at his approach. The stranger— me—was surely sent by the welfare department, and better the welfare department than the military, because then it would be too late, if it wasn't too late already. A lad, grown up fatherless, his weak, sickly mother used to beat him until he started beating her back, he shouts, smashes tables and chairs and windows, robs, pilfers, can't keep his hands off the women, and what else can I tell you about him, says the old man, Mottl is a *ganef*, a crook, small as a dwarf, but strong and wicked as the night! He's crazy, I tell you. But who, I ask you, hasn't been driven crazy in this house?

"The old man talks and talks, everything spills out of him like a shower of sparks. And I don't even get as far as Mottl Leiser, but what does it matter, do I need anything more? Of course you notice from the sly and convoluted manner of the old man that he's looking for conversation, nothing more. He tries with all the means he has at his disposal to draw you into a debate, it's as if his life depends on it, that's how much it matters to him. A stranger, too! At long last someone he hasn't said everything to already, you know, who hasn't heard it all before. How often does he have the good fortune of seeing a fresh face? He's not long for this world anyway, the old man, his bones are all crocked. And now he's trapped you, he pulls you into his room, he's wheedled a cigarette out of you, one of your good imported brand, it's a long time since he's tasted anything so good, he shuffles excitedly back and forth, lowers his voice, and tells you everything: because if he knows anything about anything, then it's this house! After Mottl Leiser he starts talking about himself. How he's lived on his own for many years, all alone like a dog. Six children scattered to the winds, oy, what am I telling you, aren't lost children your business? And his wife dying a bitter death.

"And while he speaks, the door opens and closes, faces push into the crack, all consumed with curiosity. The house is alive with noise, it hunches its back like a cat, and it listens. The house is full of murder and mayhem. Its inhabitants all work for a living, and they take it out on each other. A hard lot that forces them for twenty or thirty years to get up at four in the morning to go out into the unforgiving world on the little suburban line that is forever about to break down because of carrying so many people. And in the evenings they come home from soot-blackened factories and damp cellars, come home to their evil-smelling street and their ramshackle old house. They feel nothing anymore, they are exhausted and shattered. How long can you live that way? Eventually they crack. Each in his own way. The men get drunk and beat up their wives. The wives fall pregnant, bury their infants, and before long there's another bun in the oven. And the children, the ones that survive, they grow up crippled inside. The house, they say, that damned house sucked the life out of us! You don't believe it, asks the old man, just look at old Mrozek, a devout Christian, worked all his life, completely dried up from work, like an old stick, four children they had, two died, the youngest turns to crime. Everything they put themselves through on his account! And now? The boy goes out on the highway and commits a robbery. He almost smashes a man's skull. Just to get hold of some money. Not like his honest father, putting aside one zloty after another, over many decades, no, it has to be right away . . . And now he's behind bars, maybe he'll be let out in seven years unless he kills someone else in prison. But wonders are possible as well. Take the daughter of old Kaminska, a common prostitute, a bad woman, how did she deserve a daughter like Nina? A lily, so beautiful, God help her, a pearl, a real pearl of a daughter . . ."

And while Mendel talks in a soft and excited voice, a seeker, a *tsadek*, we've walked round the barracks I don't know how many times (I still dream of it today, the back and forth between barbed wire and watchtowers, back and forth, and when will the end come, when will we get out?), trying to avoid the suspicious glances of the guards, and once spending a quarter of an hour in the latrine.

In front of us on the perch are men puffing and groaning over their sore bellies, squatting in silence or cursing. There's a reek of chlorine, but we don't smell it, we're off somewhere else in our heads. And out we go again, casting a backward glance through the window of the wash-house. Still they're standing there praying, jerking their heads back and forth, striking their hollow chests with their hands. (They have their *taleysim* with them, and I wonder how they managed that, they were frisked four times, the jackboots took everything away from us, how did they manage to hold on to their *taleysim*?) And we walk on, and Mendel is silent. Then he stops in front of the exercise yard, and raises his arms as if in appeal, and breathes deeply and drops them again. The smell is from the cellulose factory. With its halls and chimneys, the cellulose factory looms blackly against the purplish Giant Mountains behind. Sprawled over the slope, it puffs out its yellow smoke, its sweetish toxic jaundiced fumes, into the sky. Inside, in the plant, where the smell is strongest, is where the special brigades, the chosen ones, the rich and privileged of the camp, work: it's warm in there! And we pariahs work outside in the lumberyard, where we are liable to freeze or be crushed by tree trunks. That's why the stench of the factory smells so sweet to our nostrils. It's the sweet smell of the upper class.

"What about the house then," I ask, confused, and to break the silence. "You saw all that in the house where that young man was living?"

Mendel looked at me in alarm. "I see you didn't understand anything. I talk and talk, and you understand nothing. I never was in the place where he lived. Is that so important, the house, the particular house . . . There are hidden strengths in people, but the people don't know it. They wither away, and become crippled, but still life is pressing within them. And since their pores are blocked and their eyes are blind, and they don't know what to do with all that strength, they break out. They break out of their shells, their houses, they break the law, they break out and, yes, they lash out as well . . ."

As he was speaking we were standing by the camp gates, but well concealed so that the guards outside couldn't see us. It was a Sunday and it was raining. Scraps of clouds scurried across the sky. The guards had visitors, their girls. They were laughing and flirting, chatting away happily together. We knew the guards, young beardless men, pink faces bursting with health. German farmers' sons, sons of postmen, railwaymen, and plumbers. And they were murderers. Every one of them was a murderer. They didn't know it, because we were less than human, so they had been told. They had murdered with rifle butts, with bullets, with iron bars and shovels, even with their bare hands. And now they were standing there, flirting and chatting with the girls from the village. And Mendel saw this and he looked at them, and he tried with his sad inquiring eyes, tried to understand, tried to find a phrase, a fitting word that would account for each blow, each humiliation, and each laugh at our torments, each obscene joke at our dying.

It was on one of those days that we lost Yossl. A couple of weeks before, we had received some fresh recruits: forty Jewish boys from Hungary, aged between five and fifteen, and a single Polish boy with them. And Yossl found his brother from Sosnowiec among us! We sheltered the boys, and even so they died under our protective hands. In the very first days after their arrival, some of the children died, and it was true: what were they doing here with us? Then, when Yossl keeled over at his work in the lumberyard, and the sentries shovelled snow over him as a joke, and the little heap of snow stirred and a small hand emerged from it, and they went on chucking snow over him and laughing and smoking cigarettes, and when we dragged him back to the camp that evening, then Yossl was still not yet dead. He was frozen stiff and his face was as pale as marble, and they stood around him at night in the barracks, his brother and his cousins from the little town of Sosnowiec, and they talked to him, cajoled him and flattered him and screamed at him: "Yossl, listen, you must live, Yossl, don't go, your mother is waiting, your father is waiting, Yossl, stay with us, keep us company . . ." And they stroked him and kissed him and rubbed his body with cloths and with snow, they wrapped him in blankets, and they sat him up on the table like a doll, he didn't keel over, he was frozen stiff, but he wasn't yet dead. He was frozen, but deep within him there was still a little ember of life, and they stoked it with their affectionate words, with their prayers and their charms, crying and weeping the while: "Yossl, stay!"

The rest of us, dog-tired, lay on our pallets and listened. Between dreaming and waking, we listened to their lamentations. They had got Rabbi Shimon from the next-door barracks. Rabbi Shimon covered his face and head with his *tallith* and started to pray silently. But Mendel Teichmann took hold of Yossl and shook his head disapprovingly.

"What are you wailing about, why are you crying, are you trying to scare him away with your noise? You should be happy, children, be happy as long as he's alive! Yossl is living his life now,

whether it be two hours more or twenty years, what difference
does it make, in the scope of eternity? Don't cry, children, cheer
him up, Yossl is looking at you!"

Then Pechmann was brought in. He was already asleep, but they
yanked him off his pallet and gave him a piece of bread. The western Jew Pechmann, a Vienna boy, he could make music with five
fingers on a board. How many times we had called Pechmann, and
he beat out a rhythm with his fingers on the table, he was a dab hand
at that, and we felt it through and through. With the other hand he
would hold his nose and honk like a saxophone. Blues for five fingers on a board. Now he was playing for Yossl. And the rest of us
were asleep already, and heard the playing and singing in our dark
dreams.

In the morning, as we went to work, they put Yossl in the metal
cupboard, all swaddled in blankets, the sweet marble doll, and we
trudged out into the morning darkness. In the evening, when we
came back, they took Yossl out of the cupboard, and listened to his
chest and kissed his eyelids. Yossl Kossak with the marble face. His
eyes were just barely open, but they could no longer move. He held
his hands folded across his chest, his thin, fine-boned hands, white
and shining like bone china. He wasn't dead, they swore he could
still hear them. They were quite convinced he could hear them.

Rumors circulated about the Americans, that they were about to
open a second front. But when would the second front reach us?
The Jews prayed in the wash-barracks, and besought the Almighty,
and the Christians joined in their prayer. The summer would
come, the long warm days, sunshine and the second front. Mendel
Teichmann died shortly after Yossl. He died a senseless and undig-
nified death, let me pass over it in silence. His poems are forgotten,
his ashes are scattered over the woods and fields of Poland. Mendel
Teichmann, who tried to teach me how to tell a story.

2

WHAT KEEPS
A MAN ALIVE

A man lugs rocks, lugs wood, cracks lice, fights over a potato, looks for a rusty nail by the roadside so that he can hang up his jacket on the wall at night, sews mittens out of a piece of canvas he has stolen, squeezes his sores, groans, wheezes, prays and weeps in the dark, learns to blow his nose downwind with one finger, wraps his sore feet in rags, roasts a potato after work and chews down his ration of bread. What keeps a man alive?

While he's lugging wood and cracking lice, his humiliated soul retreats into unknown depths. He views his fellow prisoners like a man fallen among wolves, only waiting for them to discover him and tear him to pieces. But inside him he is alive, he is astonished by the noble expression on the face of a dead man, or the beauty of a crystal of ice. He fills his nostrils with the smell of the woods, and he looks about him, looks for the vanished traces of beauty in his life. Suddenly he is looking for a friend with whom he can share these things, and when he has found him, he intoxicates himself with his past, spread out like an oil painting before his eyes. Something in him is driven to yell out: I am human! I have known respect! he wants to cry out. I was loved, I had a home, a wife and children, friends. I have performed kindnesses and not asked for reward. I have seen marvellous things, I know the smell of old cities. I could have done anything, achieved everything, and if I didn't do or achieve, then it was only because I didn't know, I couldn't sense . . . He wants to shout all that, he wants to dazzle, to boast, to talk himself breathless. He can't, he doesn't have the words, he doesn't have the art. But that's what keeps a man alive, the fact that the dream of his lost beautiful life, of freedom and purity of heart, is not yet at an end.

He begins to talk, haltingly, cautiously remonstrating with the other. It might be de Groot, say, who spoke: "You can tell me I lived like a fool, that I was a snob, a bloody stuck-up snob. All right, I tell you, you're right. But I was alive. Deeply alive . . ." He blows warm air into his hands, which are white and half frozen, then he smacks them against his thighs, and he runs back and forth so as not to freeze, the little tailor from Amsterdam. How does he do it, I ask myself, where does he get the strength, this little starved wizened fellow—when I see big strong men fall down every day.

The work is going slowly today, it is bitterly cold. The conveyor belt is empty, there is a mechanical fault in the sawing plant. No guards to be seen anywhere, they are all off sheltering somewhere. We can hear the Red Rooster crowing in the hall. He is shouting and yelling, as if he is pleased that everything has ground to a halt, so he can shout and lash out. Two or three comrades, laden with long planks, come past, listen to de Groot, and roll their eyes. They've heard it all seven times: the lovely Amsterdam afternoons, five o'clock at Kroon's café on the Rembrandtsplein, or Heck's or Huisman's in Kalverstraat. Rikje and himself. She was just as small and tough as him. They could eat and drink whatever they felt like. Delicious chocolate éclairs with cream, or a truffled veal chop in the grill of the Hotel Trianon. They didn't put on the weight. And they smoked like ship's chimneys, cigars, cigarillos, pipe, yes, his wife too. For her fortieth birthday, he bought her a meerschaum pipe on a weekend away in London, at Heester's or Pleester's or whatever the name of the shop was. Then they strolled down the street full of antique shops, on the lookout for an agate ashtray or an old English etching. The worries those people had!

"In the evenings," de Groot continues unabashed, "we would take a constitutional down the length of the Kalverstraat as far as the Dam, then along Damrak to the Central Station, and back to

Rembrandtsplein. We could never have enough of seeing the young people, the pretty girls, the young bucks, if you take my meaning. We would drink a cognac at Heck's, before going on to a little restaurant known to insiders, behind the Portuguese synagogue, where people dined on Russian-Jewish, Polish or Moorish specialities in hat and slippers, among humming samovars in candlelight. The curiosity, the plain silly curiosity with which we stuck our noses in everywhere! And the swarms of people in the narrow lanes beside the canals, in the little bars and artists' cafés. How they thronged together, and talked and talked! There's no other way of saying it. Life was beautiful."

They had mingled with a theatre crowd, he told us, with clairvoyants, émigré princes, nightclub owners, and famed assassins on their way to Paris. The talk they heard was royally entertaining; they were astonished by the mental acrobatics of petty adventurers seeking to raise money for some invention or piece of information or other. He and Rikje had no children, they didn't know what worries were.

"All right," said de Groot, "you'll call us blind. Very well, I say, you're right. No, we really didn't have a clue what was going on in the world. We didn't listen to the warnings of our friends: 'Pack your belongings,' they urged us, 'go to America!' We didn't believe the horrible news from Germany, we had always admired and respected the Germans. We thought it was exaggerated talk, as you do, perhaps from people who had something to gain. We were happy. Perhaps we didn't want to see or hear anything else."

"You thought only of yourself," said Chukran, who had come over and joined us. He didn't want to offend de Groot; he said it with a smile. Chukran always smiled, twisted his joker's face into a grimace so that, whatever he said, no one could be angry with him. But de Groot was angry now, or pretended he was.

"What do you mean, I thought only of myself!" he cried. "I gave alms all my life, I must have fed half a dozen writers and artists.

Everyone who needed money came to de Groot. What more should I have done?"

"You know what I mean," said Chukran, still smiling. "None of us did what we should have done."

We were stunned, we hadn't heard that sort of talk from him before. "There were people who took steps," said Chukran, "and they're, you know, still alive today."

"But what did they achieve?" asked de Groot. "Nothing!"

"Today we can't appreciate it," said Chukran, "but maybe tomorrow. What they have done or are doing as we speak—our children will see it."

The tailor made a contemptuous gesture and was about to go on. But then the Red Rooster came running up, shouting to us that we weren't to stand around, we had to work, throwing lengths of wood onto the conveyor belt, and sharpish, or he'd show us. The Red Rooster, a so-called ethnic German by the name of Kramer, seventy years old, with a face invariably purple with rage, with spindly limbs in continual hectic movement, twitching or lashing out with a hoarse cry, like the crowing of an old rooster—we laughed at him and were afraid of him, and were careful to look busy whenever he came running up. De Groot from Amsterdam handed me some wood from the great stack the night shift had unloaded. I passed it on to Chukran from Tours, Chukran handed it to Modche Rabinowicz from Krakow, who gave it to Feinberg from Paris, and Feinberg threw it on the conveyor belt, which had already transported whole forests to the chopping plant of the Phrixa cellulose factory in the Giant Mountains, where it was reduced to tiny shavings.

"A Jew can't come to money in Tours," said Chukran, the moment the Red Rooster had turned his back on us to dignify other inmates with his attention. Chukran wanted to get in ahead of de Groot, and tell his own story. "I tell you," said Chukran with a mocking smile, "a Turkish Jew, a *Terk*, who has ended up in Tours, he needs to pack his kitbag with sheets and towels, with silk scarves, aprons and cotton shirts, and try his luck in the weekly markets in the outlying villages. Upstanding Christian men and women live in Tours. People there give each other the time of day, and they ask after the children, and they act respectful, but nothing more. Not that I experienced anti-Semitism there, God forbid, but you have to keep your distance, those are the rules. At least that's what Miriam wanted."

Miriam, his wife, was the daughter of a Jewish baker in Paris, who had emigrated there from his native Poland. The sweet girl had been well brought up, playing the piano and speaking foreign languages. As well as Yiddish, Polish, and French, all of them so to speak her mother tongues, she could speak English and Italian. Chukran explained: "To begin with, she was dead against me. What's a common *Terk*, a peddler Jew, a travelling salesman, to a lady like Miriam? Well, I bided my time patiently. Her father died soon. Her mother carried on the business with three partners, Yids with no sense. Miriam was thinking in terms of a doctor, a gentleman with a degree. Bakers, traders, Jewish tailors and furriers from the street aren't good enough for her. God forbid, am I about to push myself forward? I always came as a friend, a *khaver*, and asked her how she was doing, helped the mother run the business, order the stock, keep the books, collect the debts. I bought wood because they had to extend the shop, I advised on dough-mixing equipment, modern ovens . . . The woman saw how a *Terk*, a coarse and uncultured market Jew, can be a good provider! Well, and Miriam grew accustomed to me. Three years I waited for her 'yes' to come. Then she wanted to leave Paris. She was ashamed of me, because I wasn't refined or distinguished. Every day I drove from village to village in the truck. But then she gave me a son and a daughter, and another son, and Miriam forgot her *khaloymes*, her girlish dreams. But she remained a lady, a bourgeoise! In Tours, I could never go out unshaven, and only in a collar and tie. And not talk business with anyone . . ."

There was another mechanical breakdown in the hall. If we weren't loading the conveyor belt, we still weren't allowed to do nothing; we had to stack the lengths of wood in tidy piles. The Red Rooster had run to the chopping plant on his stick legs. And Chukran fell to pondering for a few moments. De Groot took advantage of the pause to pick up his own thread. Meanwhile, the lengths of wood were passed from hand to hand. Each time we kept hold of them for an instant longer to save strength and not stand there with empty hands, in case a guard unexpectedly showed up.

"Never worked a day longer than five hours," said the tailor. "Four suits a month, one a week, never more! You couldn't get rich on it, well I'll give you that, you're right. But you made yourself scarce, the product rose in value, my suits were like a brand if you take my meaning. Well then, why should I work any harder, and put aside money in the bank? Who for? I'd be a fool. I had the best customers in the Netherlands, and some of them even had crests on the automobiles they drove up in!"

It took protection to get a suit tailored by de Groot. The Duke of Windsor had ordered evening dress from him, that's how far his fame had spread. A suit from de Groot of Amsterdam! Each production a masterpiece, fitting a man's profile, expressing his particular quality, his character, his caste, his class. Understatement, dignity, elegance! "I could have employed fifteen assistants," said de Groot, "but then my label would have been finished. I would have become rich, an outfitter . . ."

Chukran laughed aloud, then his laugh turned into a cry of pain. The Red Rooster had snuck up on, and aimed a kick at, the Turk. He was practiced at finding a victim's testicles with the toe of his boot. As the unhappy man rolled around on the ground in pain, the Red Rooster proceeded to kick him in the belly and kidneys. The only thing that helped was to create a diversion; someone had to upset the stack of wood. Then, snorting with fury, the Red Rooster would turn on the new victim. Further tricks had to be employed to draw the devil on further and further down the conveyor belt, into the chopping plant. Those halls were warm, and we thought anyone working there would be well-fed and strong and better able to deal with that madman. For those of us outside, in the cold, in the lumberyard, it meant a couple of minutes of respite, a chance to swear and catch our breath and inhale the pure wood smell, as though the Red Rooster gave off poisonous fumes. You could go and piss behind a stack of logs or hunker down on a tree trunk for a minute, close your eyes and reflect, while a comrade stood watch.

Chukran was pale after his blow. His testicles were already swollen from previous kicks. Thick tears of rage and helplessness dribbled down his puffy clown's face. When he had got over the cramp, he got up, shook his head, and sent a stream of wild curses in the direction of his tormentor. Then he was silent, collecting himself. He stood upright, the strongest among us, a giant, while the rest of us were already Muselmen.*

Then he said calmly, in Yiddish: "Why does he beat Jews? What is an old man like that doing here anyway, why doesn't he stay home and drink coffee? What have they done to him? He doesn't know them. Perhaps he knows one who kept a store in his village. Perhaps he knows another one who was a doctor. They only knew the rich Jews. And when he hears 'They're not people, beat them!' he beats them. Because he's stupid. Maybe he felt sorry the first time he did it. But his fear of not obeying is greater than his compassion. If you are fearful and envious, then you will hate the Jews. After he threw the first blow he threw the second, because he knows what he's doing is wrong and he wants to silence that inner

*Concentration-camp slang for a prisoner who is patently doomed.

voice that says, 'Stop it, it's wrong.' And so he beats and beats. God help him die quickly. The shorter the life, the less the sin.' "

The silhouettes of two sentries loomed against the evening light. We stacked lengths of wood. Chukran, our best worker, tossed the wood so that it was a pleasure to behold; he wasn't saving any of his strength. The jackboots stomped off, satisfied. I looked at Chukran. You could be years with a prisoner and not know him. The common *Terk*, the peddler Jew, the joker and strong man, the wisecracker and wiseacre, the man of violence and barbarian (if it was a matter of fighting for his survival), had revealed yet another side of himself. The sun faded behind a bank of clouds. We waited impatiently for the end of the working day. Hot soup beckoned. Our pallets and our rest seemed to us all the happiness in the world. But after the end of work we faced the hour-long march back to camp, dragging ourselves along in our sodden clogs, and singing all the while, forever the same Polish songs. Those songs, the smoke from the huts spreading over the white fields, the sadness of the landscape, how beautiful it all was! The hanging heads of our comrades, almost asleep on their feet, immersed in reveries. Hunger and exhaustion had dulled them. But that dullness was a fertile ground for feverish inner pictures. To speak to a man on the march was to shatter the spell. To utter a clear sentence, analyze our situation, or even wring a poem from a dulled brain, to change the words of a song and turn them subtly into something rebellious, who could do such a thing? Never more than a handful of men in each army.

In the middle of our column we carried the sick and feeble back into camp, as we did every evening. This time, among others, it was Modche Rabinowicz. As we marched out at dawn, Modche had sung:

Ot azoy, ot asoy,
Iz gekumen Reyzl's khosn,
Ot azoy, ot azoy . . .*

And then, in Yiddish, almost beside himself, "Children, when we're home again Mama will bless the candles, and Papa will kiss the *hallah* bread . . . We will remember today forever."

He sang and did a shuffling dance, a sudden burst of joy and exuberance spilled out of him. Then, when we got to our place of work, he collapsed and suddenly couldn't breathe, lashed out spastically with hands and feet. We hid him in a toolshed. We looked in on him during our short midday break and were shocked: he had rolled about on the sacks of chalk and was powdered white and ghostly, like a figure from a Japanese legend, a sculpture. When he caught sight of us, he started to cry in a stifled voice, "I'm dying, I'm dying, water, I'm dying . . ."

Someone brought him water, I remember, it was Jacques. And when Rabinowicz started yelling and kicking again it was Jacques who held him tight and said, "What are you shouting like that for, man, why are you making so much noise? You're not dying. We're not going to die, we're going to live. They're going to die . . ."

Rabinowicz was no longer in his right mind, he didn't understand what the Frenchman was saying to him. But we who witnessed it, we understood. In the evening, when we assembled, Rabinowicz was dead.

But now I must tell about Jacques: a Parisian laborer and resistance fighter. A bold character, lovable, cheeky, cheerful, and full of rage. There was a compelling logic about his life story. "When I was fifteen," he used to say, "all I cared about was girls and a hundred

*Just like that, just like that,
  Reyzl's bridegroom came . . .

schemes for making money." But when he was seventeen, Jacques found himself on the boulevard in a workers' demonstration, and was baton-charged along with the others. The *flics* all but broke his skull; from then on, he attended every rally. When the Spanish Civil War began, Jacques set off for Madrid with the first wave of volunteers. He was wounded several times, and when it was all over he was interned in France. When the Germans occupied the south of France, Jacques joined the Maquis.* His group of partisans were betrayed by a spy, five comrades were shot. It was pure chance that he avoided their fate.

Wherever Jacques went, he gave us lessons in the struggle. One Sunday they got prisoners to unload a wagon. Two strong men climbed onto it, to hand down the heavy slabs of concrete. The rest of us had to carry them to the construction site. Haase, the Kapo,† continually urged us to make haste; the guard was new, it was his first time in a camp. We noticed the edginess in his look. A new man was always dangerous. What would he do? The Kapos tried to test him by flattering him and driving us on. We were afraid of the new man, and he was afraid of us, afraid of getting entangled in an unfamiliar situation.

With poorly concealed curiosity he watched us at work. One of the prisoners was too feeble to carry the heavy concrete slabs, so we gave him a wooden pole or a broken-off fragment of concrete instead. Slowly and menacingly the guard approached. Still slightly uncertain, he eyed the unhappy individual. He grabbed the wooden pole from him and pointed to a piece of concrete tubing at least a hundred pounds in weight.

"There, pick that up, you Jewish pig, or else you'll catch it."

---

*The French Resistance to Nazi occupation, derived from the name for the scrubland of Corsica and southeast France, where some of its early members operated.
†A Kapo (from the Italian *capo*, "head") was the prisoner in charge of a labor brigade. Later used to describe all prisoners given any authority.

The prisoner tried to pick up the tubing, but he couldn't move it.

"Pick it up!" yelled the jackboot, his voice trembling with awkwardness and rage.

The prisoner, a Jewish schoolmaster from Holland, was too weak to stand. He squatted on the ground, with his head hanging in despair. "Pick it up!" screamed the SS man again and again, casting uncertain looks about him. He realized how futile it was, but he couldn't go back. His hand moved to his holster . . .

Then Jacques walked quickly up to the man squatting on the ground, barged him contemptuously aside, and called out, "Fool! No marrow in your bones." We all knew whom he really meant. "Look here, Muselman," he said, "this is the way it's done!"

He shouldered the tubing and carried it off. The sick man slunk along behind him, while the jackboot stared after them, speechless. Then he grinned foolishly, and stalked off in relief.

Jacques always knew exactly what to do. On the way to work, we heard him singing French and Spanish revolutionary songs, whose magic made us strong and angry. The guard probably sensed the effect on us, but he couldn't understand the words.

"Hey, you bastard!" the guard shouts. "What's that filth you're singing?"

"Filth," the singer replied brazenly, "that's Spanish filth, you sons of bitches!" And added a long and incomprehensible curse. There was a diabolical grin on his face.

The guard, to mask his defeat, ran up and waved his rifle butt at the column. "Wake up, you shitbags, march! I'll show you!"

But Jacques too fell ill and had fits of weakness. Then he would talk little and drag himself along at the end of his strength. Sometimes when we had the sense that he was about to keel over, we were wrong, and he didn't. We heard him emit gruff sounds with every groan and sigh. "Taras, *je viens, tu verras, ne t'en fais pas* . . ." I'm coming back, you'll see, don't worry, I'll be back. Then—Reval—

you'll be sorry about Serge, Antonopolo, Maurice . . . He listed the names, even at night in his sleep we heard him listing the names without a mistake: the name of the traitor and those of the victims. Like a prayer.

Jacques saved his strength, never worked without using his sharp eyes to see how much work needed to be done, for this Kapo, for that guard, so as not to draw attention to himself for zeal or idleness. Like me and Chukran and a few others, he sewed caps and mittens from scraps of found or stolen cloth, in the evenings, when most of the men were already asleep. It took effort not to let yourself sink into sleep, but instead to keep your eyes open and make something that the Kapos and the *Prominenten** in the camp would buy, for soup or bread. Jacques kept himself clean, didn't eat grass or trash, kept an eye on his small wounds. It was more than an ordinary vengefulness that made him struggle for each and every breath.

"I don't hate him," Jacques answered once, when I asked him. "Why should I hate him, a cockroach you stamp on . . . But five men on his conscience, you understand . . . I could have prevented it, if I'd been more suspicious. I knew he was weak! And now he's waiting for me. He's afraid of me, he can hardly bear to wait for me. He knows I'm coming for him. He's yelling for me . . ."

His inflamed eyes glittered as he spoke. A vast tiredness and a powerful will were struggling within him. Chukran lived because he wanted to live, Jacques because he had to kill. Mendel Teichmann lived with his eyes, the eyes of the *tsadek*, the wise man, who saw everything. The ones who survived were the fulfilled ones, who wanted to drain their lives to the very last drop—even if it was a cup of poison. The dream wasn't yet at an end.

---

*Collective term for inmates in positions of authority or who worked in kitchens, laundry, or artisanal workshops; they were often hated as much as the SS.

3

BREAD

To eat bread, all you need is a little slab of fresh wood. You can find wood like that pretty much anywhere. Wood stands for forest, clearing, underbrush. It signifies house, shelter, comfort. All that's lost. Put it on the ground, on a pallet, on your knee, and you have a clean table. It signals to you that you're at home, where you live. And now the bread: divide it up into three thick slices, break the slices into cubes. Chew each cube long and thoroughly. Taste the grain in it, the rain, the storm. Let the taste of the sun dissolve on your tongue.

Bread is life. He who steals bread from another man steals his life. Kemal the Turk stole bread. Who denounced him? Once, as we were returning to the barracks from work, there's someone hanging suspended. They've tied his feet to the roof beam. Manasse Rubinstein, our youngest Kapo, is standing behind him, swinging the whip. The criminal makes no sound—is he unconscious? Manasse Rubinstein wears rings on his white fingers, he wears boots, the emblem of the ruling class, and a fantasy uniform sewn for him by Jewish tailors. Is it about the bread? What is the charge against Kemal? Do they, the Kapos, not steal our bread on a daily basis? A lock of Manasse Rubinstein's black hair has slipped down over his eyes as a result of his exertions. Manasse is a handsome man. The angel with the whip. And he metes out the punishment—whatever punishment he is called upon to mete out—coolly, dispassionately. Afterward he washes his hands and lights a cigarette.

Most of the prisoners eat their bread right away. They tear it apart with their hands and gulp down the pieces with the greed of mortal exhaustion. Also, that way no one can steal it from them. There is a loaf of bread between six men, sometimes eight—on

rare, good days, one between four! And what governs that? A few
scholiasts claim to be able to tell the state of the fronts from the size
of the bread allocation. When the allocation is bigger, that means
the Allies are advancing and the Nazis are being beaten back, and
dreading the rage of the world. Others argue the very opposite.

So the bread comes, the six men crawl into a corner, and go
about the sacred business of dividing it up. There are various meth-
ods. For example, the drawing of lots. The loaf is quickly hacked
into six unequal pieces and lots are drawn for the pieces with numbers on a scrap of paper. It's the same odds for everyone, no one
can complain. Whoever has drawn the biggest piece tries to mask
his delight, so as not to offend his comrades. He picks it up quickly
and disappears under his blanket with it. Whoever has drawn the
smallest also goes to bed, but because only sleep can comfort him.
It's when you wake up that hunger, cold, and all the Biblical
plagues of the livelong day assail you. The normal way of dividing
bread is like this: a horizontal piece of wood suspended on a piece
of string, two cones on the ends, these are pushed into the bread,
and the pieces are elaborately weighed until all the rations are
identical. This method has the advantage of taking a long time,
which means the bread is still being weighed while others have
already eaten theirs. As the bread crumbles in the course of being
divided and weighed, everyone holds their caps underneath it to
catch the crumbs. Then I still have to mention the masochists, the
members of a secret bread cult. They torment themselves with an
illusion. They put their ration into a bag they carry with them at
all times. The bread, existing outside of their bodies instead of
inside, might sustain their imaginations, but it robs them of their
strength. They die faster than the others. In the course of working,
who knows when, usually unseen by the others, they pull out tiny
scraps—their elixir—from their bags, and eat them. Idiots. And
then there are the men like Pechmann and others who turn a crust
of bread into a seven-course meal, who sit down, produce their

carefully treasured piece of board, and feast. Mendel Teichmann
laughs at them. Mendel Teichmann the lion tears the bread in
pieces and stuffs it in his mouth, at least once a day. As for those
other people—ridiculous! That's what squirrels do, rodents, rumi-
nants. Lambs nibble.

· A year on, I see him, too, Mendel Teichmann, the *tsadek*, the
magician with words, eat up his bread ration with board and knife.
People everywhere change their minds, why not here? As Mendel
Teichmann feels his strength ebb away, he, once the lion, discovers
the small joys of the lamb. Bread. Taste the grain in it, the rain, the
storm. Let the taste of the sun dissolve on your tongue.

4

A SENSE OF
PARADISE

For four days the battle had been raging. At night we could see the fire in the eastern sky. The prisoners listened to the sounds with lips pressed together, as if it was the coming of the Messiah. The Red Army had reached Auschwitz, we heard. And then uncertainty and silence and the indifferently falling snow that covered everything. One day, carts and wagons stood outside the camp. Ladder wagons, old carriages, hay carts, even a couple of bright red fire wagons from the days when the fire brigade used horse-drawn appliances. There were no horses.

Rabbi Shimon shook his head. "Surely they won't expect us to . . ." But we pulled the wagons. A thousand prisoners. We pulled them up the snowy mountains as if we had never done anything else. The ice cracked under the wheels. SS Oberscharführer Wenzel, a handsome man, had got hold of a horse from somewhere, and he galloped back and forth, commanding our caravan. What a sight, that strong beast, wound up like a steel spring, picking its way uncertainly over the ice, with taut neck and blood-veined eyes.

Every wagon was being pulled by twenty or thirty groaning Jews. Breath froze in tiny crystals. A few sang, others cried, swore, prayed—no one paid them any attention in the general noise. Lubitsch declaimed French poetry. He pulled on a rope, set one foot in front of the other on the icebound earth, and recited Baudelaire. Rabbi Shimon suddenly came down with cramps. They put him behind a cart to help prop him up. Because anyone who couldn't go on was given a bullet. Feinberg the tailor got his bullet soon, and the little man from Budiach. The Giant Mountains rang with gunshots, the sky was mild and blue. The first dead lay by the roadside, but the march over the mountains had only just begun. On this road, where once Polish armies had ridden against the Turks, there were now Jewish tailors, grocers, and doctors, lying like dummies in strange contortions, only a moment ago they had been moving.

From a farm across the street, a little girl watched the spectacle. The door was open behind her, and swathes of steam came wafting out. Half hidden behind a tree, the girl watched the long column. She had her sleeves rolled up, her healthy red arms were steaming, the trough full of laundry was steaming at her feet. For an instant I was overcome by memories of the various smells of soap and clean shirts, bread and onions and barley coffee. It was good to know they still existed somewhere.

> O grandest of the angels, and most wise,
> O fallen God, fate-driven from the skies,
> Satan, at last take pity on our pain.
>
> O first of exiles who endurest wrong,
> Yet growest, in thy hatred, still more strong,
> Satan, at last take pity on our pain.*

Lubitsch declaimed the poem with eyes shut, as though in fever. Perhaps he did have a fever. Rabbi Shimon allowed his head to droop, we knew we wouldn't be able to save him. His nephew, Kalischer, the tiny dwarf Moische Kalischer with the big head that had no clarity in it, who had told me everything while we were working in the lumberyard, all about their beloved little town of Sosnowiec where they had lived, about his mother and seven brothers, and their miserly uncle—now he pressed himself against his uncle, because he was the only one left, while all the others were rotting in the ground. And Moische Kalischer cried. He too had cramps. Many had sudden cramps. All who had eaten potatoes

*Baudelaire, "Litanies de Satan," trans. James Elroy Flecker.

that morning, fighting over them just as we were setting out, hot potatoes boiled in stinking water, they all now came down with cramps. And Kalischer stepped aside to void his bowels. That's where he got his bullet. The shot felled him like a blow from a club. Meanwhile, the world still contained little girls with pink cheeks and steaming hands, who washed clothes and knew nothing about anything, and who hid at the sight of us. It still contained rooms with wood-paneled walls in old farmhouses, where the good smell of fresh bread, onions, and barley coffee had taken refuge.

> *Race of Abel, eat, sleep and feed,*
> *God is pleased;*
> *grovel in the dirt and die,*
> *Race of Cain.*
> *Race of Abel, your sacrifice*
> *flatters the nostrils of the Seraphim;*
> *Race of Cain, is your punishment*
> *never to know an end?*
> *Race of Abel, your fields prosper,*
> *your cattle grow fat;*
> *Race of Cain, your belly clamors*
> *like a famished dog.**

I knew the lines. For years I had listened to Lubitsch declaiming them. He said he knew seven hundred lines of poetry by heart. Lubitsch came from an old Jewish patrician family that owned several sugar factories and large estates in Slovakia. He could speak French better than any other language, and that was before he had emigrated to France. Before long, he had found a very good job there. There was no better qualification for a job in Paris, he had told

*Baudelaire, "Abel et Cain," trans. Richard Howard.

us, than a mastery of French. Lubitsch was a pederast, but who cared about that. He accepted the greatest sufferings and tribulations with a stoicism that no one could understand. His world was poetry and higher mathematics. He rarely met with anyone he could talk with on equal terms, so on free days he would look for a piece of paper and fill it with rows of figures and mysterious formulae. His strength was fading, his face and hands were disfigured by swellings. But he still refused to acknowledge the evil in the world.

There was a sharp turn in the road. Several carts had come to grief there, crashing against old trees below. Crates and sacks lay scattered about, some had come open and spilled their contents. We could see silver Sabbath candelabra, copper kettles, samovars, furs, piles of damask linen, even a spinet. The jackboots yelled at the prisoners to gather up the boxes and sacks. But all the carts were already overloaded, and every jackboot was looking after his own booty. There they were now with their crates and their sacks, the robbers, biting their lips. There were dead bodies among the ruined carts as well. Thin streams of purple colored the snow.

The paper cement sack I wore against my skin creaked with every step. I had turned up the collar of my striped jacket and pressed my cheek against it. It was warm there. If Pechmann had still been alive, he would have gone flitting from man to man, whispering, "Keep going, children, not much longer. The Germans are frightened, believe me, I know. There are partisans waiting on the Czech side of the border . . ." Blinking nervously with his naive eyes, which brightened at moments in fits of confused hope, he would have tried to encourage us and himself. Ever since we had known him, he had picked up on every rumor or report that promised any turn in our fate. Perhaps like all of us he could see the catastrophe looming, but he didn't want to see it. Till the very last moment, he was waiting for a miracle. Even in death he had a smile on his thin blue lips and a childish expression of surprise, as if he didn't quite believe it.

But Pechmann was no longer with us. Nor was Chukran, the strongest of us, the Turkish-Jewish trader from Tours in France. I was lying at the time in the sick-barracks, because I was spitting blood. Almost all my comrades in the sick-barracks were spitting blood. That morning, Chukran was still joking in his familiar way, making us laugh with his grimaces—not without its dangers if you were spitting blood. One of us choked to death from a hemorrhage incurred from laughing. That night, Chukran's best friend Lemberger had died. We had all been waiting for it to happen. Lemberger had stopped eating several days previously; his salivary glands had failed, he was no longer able to swallow. But Chukran was still eating, and no one thought he could die.

Well, early in the morning, the prisoners' doctor and Karel, the nurse, were looking at the dead man. Chukran pulled his broad joker's face. "You'll see, doctor, it's my turn next!" The doctor and Karel grinned and shook their heads. Toward noon, Chukran got quieter and quieter. As it grew dark outside, he lay down flat on his back, pulled a leather wallet out of his tattered shirt (none of us still had anything like a wallet—how had he managed to pull that off?), took out a photo of his wife and four children as well as a couple of letters and mementos, looked at them calmly, put them back in the wallet, handed it to his neighbor, Jacques, who was convinced he would see Paris again when it was all over, and said, "Send this to my wife." And then his face turned black.

The road wound its way among precipitous drops, through ancient forests smothered in snow. Clinging onto the carts were men who no longer had any sensation in their feet, and were hoping merely to extend their lives by an hour or so. But they kept dropping to their knees behind the carts. The jackboots would grab them like so many sacks of potatoes and drag them to the roadside. A bang and an echo and nothing else, not even a scream. The sun sank in thick mist, mist tinted pink, then red, orange, and blue. More mountains loomed in front of us. A Jew next to me by the axle, a man I didn't know, large, bony, and stooped, his face extinguished, kept murmuring with every breath, "How much longer? How much longer? How much longer?" He kept his eyes shut, his hands, which were ripped and bloody from the axle, kept pulling the wagon, we all were pulling the wagon, the wagon was our life, the wagon was a game, whoever succeeded in getting it across the mountains had won.

Then it got dark, and the banging from the rifles stopped. Now they just pushed the victims over the edge, and left them to die of cold. We spent the night in an erstwhile sawmill. Suddenly, miraculously, the old building loomed out of the fog. We collapsed onto mounds of fragrant sawdust, as into a lovely feather bed. Outside the open window casements, bullets hissed by to warn us. The men screamed in their sleep, groaned with twisted mouths. A couple of dozen men failed to get up in the morning. The groans had been their last. Their sleep, their deep sleep, had dragged them down. We couldn't help them; we envied them.

During the descent on the Czech side, the wagons began to slide. Dragging them uphill had been torture, but downhill was infernal. Not until four or five wagons had gone over the side did we learn how to brake them. We looked out thick branches from the side of the road. Whoever was still with us might have a chance. In front of us lay the valley, the column of vehicles made its way downhill with a deafening din. The soldiers yelled, swung their rifle butts at the heads of the prisoners if progress was too fast and a cart threatened to go over the edge. Their faces were purple with rage. Others, who had already seen their vehicles go, walked on empty-handed and no longer yelling. Silently they trudged along behind us, sensing illumination.

"Get back, away from the axle!" yelled one of the men who still had some strength into the ear of a weakling. "Hold on, Litvak, hold tight, the road's going to get steeper!"

Litvak's name was Sasha. The fact that the eastern Jews in the camp called him Litvak was a kind of acknowledgment of his Lithuanian origins. But he came from Brussels, and who he really was, and what was going on within him, only I could guess. I knew him from the transport, and from the platform at Birkenau. The doors had been opened, and the SS men yelled out, "The men out! All the men out!" There was wild confusion in the car, as women and children clung tearfully to their men. A few half-drunk jackboots broke it up with swinging fists and revolver butts. "All the men out!" Sasha gently loosened the hands of his beautiful wife from his neck; the children—adorable little fair-haired angels—he firmly and tenderly prised away from his legs. It had to be. Outside, one of the Germans had already slaughtered a child, and was laughing with hard eyes. I was down on the platform with the other unmarried men, looking up. It seemed to me I had never seen such a beautiful woman. Then Sasha was standing beside me, stepping up to the martial sound of a tango. The music of the prisoners' orchestra drowned out the cries of the children. Slowly the train rolled on, in the direction of some tall chimneystacks. Sasha watched it go. He didn't know what would happen there. We all didn't know, though we feared the worst. And now, years later, there he was staggering behind a cart, almost in his death agony. He didn't complain, he had never talked that much anyway, his eyes were directed within. I knew what they saw. Only I, who had watched before, knew.

In the evening hours, we saw the town below us. Lily-white was the sky above, lights dotted about the slopes like occasional stars. The outskirts of Reichenberg. Snowflakes began to fall, and muffled the noise. Men stood on the road like statues, not moving. I looked back at Sasha. But Sasha was no longer there.

5

THE
SEVENTH
WELL

The men no longer talk. Almost a week ago, in the Giant Mountains, when there was still food, a loaf of bread each and a can of meat, which we gulped down, and snow to moisten our lips, then you could still hear the croaky voices. Now their lips are dried. They talk only to themselves, in fever, in death agony. A few have come home, and are talking to their loved ones. They tell them stories, ask questions, soothe, and sweet-talk. When the train moves, the murmurs and death rattles are drowned out by the clattering of the wheels.

The train has been going for several days now. Sometimes it stops overnight on a siding near a bridge that civilians hurry across, casting nervous glances down at it. Open wagons stuffed full of men, bent double with cold. Only when they die do they stretch out in something resembling dignity. There lies Meir Bernstein, half rigid, but his eyes are open and staring intently. What does he see? Not Perez and Berkowicz at his feet, waiting for him. Because he has good shoes, the farmer Meir Bernstein, and a warm jacket of cellulose. What does a dead farmer want with shoes and a jacket? They bide their time.

Meir Bernstein looks past them. He sees his wife Chanah, and he sees the five children. They are sitting at the festive table, the mother has lit two candles, and covered her head with a white cloth. She closes her eyes to pray, then she *bentsches*, she blesses the candles, the fragrant honey-colored *hallah*,* which they are about to break, blesses the heads of the children, and Meir Bernstein smiles in delight and he thinks, Chanah, he thinks, Chanele, I am

*Sabbath bread.

back on the Sabbath, I knew I would be back with you by Passover. So he thinks. How do I know? Because he often used to talk about Sabbath at his house, the rich farmer Meir Bernstein. All eastern Jews like to talk about holidays. But they are not talking now. They are dreaming. No more true stories from a life that will never come back, no more Hasidic sophistries, *bonkes* and memories; this is a train in which there are nothing but dreams, fever dreams, crazy dreams till a man's dying breath. A dream train rolling through the dark forests of Germany. Dreams from melancholy-bold Warsaw and sun-baked Provence, dreams from Vienna and Paris, and from the black coal pits of Charleroi. I know the stories of the dead who lie on the outer platform of the wagons. I know the stories of Meir Bernstein, he told them many times. His lips are moving, he is whispering something. Perhaps a prayer in thanks? "Thank you, Almighty," he whispers into the cold air, "thank you for letting me see my Chanah and the children once more, thank you, *reboyne-sheloylem*."

Then the train rumbles over a set of points, disturbs his dream. It brakes with a shrill squeal. It will come to another stop, in the middle of nowhere. The sentries will leap out onto the embankment and stretch their legs and laugh with gruff voices and call out to one another. The locomotive will whistle and demand to be allowed to pass, but it will have to stay there for a long time and puff and snort, like a captive giant. Just like yesterday, close by a German station, when suddenly Chaim Jitzchok swung himself over the side, little sixteen-year-old Chaim Jitzchok, and started running. Silly boy, why don't you think before you act? First, it's all quiet, we hold our breath and listen, then there's banging and popping from all sides. They're playing with him, like a cat with a mouse, pretending to let him go. Chaim must have lost his mind, now he's offering them a pastime. Again, we hear the sadistic soldiers' voices, they're driving the victim to his death. Chaim Jitzchok is running across a boggy field, he creeps behind a spindly birch tree, which is immediately cut down by bullets, he runs on, the rope round his waist comes undone, his pants slip down; he falls in a puddle, the ice breaks with a ring like a bell. Thunderous laughter. The train slowly moves off, there is no more time, they give him a bullet in the neck. Silence.

Today too the locomotive snorts and puffs, it makes an almost human wail, the sentries stamp their feet on the sodden sleepers. Two or three prisoners reach over the boards to try and pull a bit of snow off some fir twigs. The jackboots yell, "Get down, you Jew pigs, or we'll shoot you!" And the men jump back. Never again will they feel moisture on their lips. They die silently. Only Meir Bernstein raises his head, angry and a little astonished. Perez and Berkowicz are waiting at his feet, they seem almost to be listening to his thoughts. Those plebs always listened in a kind of numbness when Meir Bernstein told his stories—with the pride and condescension of a rich farmer who has fifty cows in his sheds, and who rules over vast acres. And Meir tells his stories with artful embellishments, almost like Mendel Teichmann and others who have been persecuted for centuries, and who have learned to live by the word.

"*Hert mikh oys*," Meir Bernstein likes to begin, "*vel ikh aykh dertseyln a mayse* . . . I want to tell you a story: It was on a Sabbath, and everyone knew that the Sabbath is a holy day, a *yontev*, in the house of Meir Bernstein. Now, Meir Bernstein was never one of those Jews who stuck to the letter of the laws of the Talmud. Devout, yes, but the spirit, not the letter! Because God lives in me and you and every shrub and tree, and is bigger than a letter, so I too am bigger than a letter. But Shabbes is Shabbes. No light is lit by my hand, horse and cart remain in their stable. Then on Friday evening a peasant comes by, a Christian. Not a bad man, but he's had a bit to drink, and he wants to prove to me I'm a *meshumed* and no Yid at all! 'Meir,' he says to me, 'Meir, get your horse and cart and come with me. The weir is closed, and it can hardly hold the swollen stream, and if you don't open the gate, the meadow will be flooded.' I go out to fetch the farmhand. But the farmhand is sprawled out in the straw, drunk on schnapps. I put the horse to, and we ride out to the weir. Ignoble people gave schnapps to the farmhand, and shut off the weir. I open it with my own hands, the goy watches me, surprised I don't ask him to do it for me. Then as we're riding back through the village, he says, 'Come in and have a drink with me.' Well, he's deserved a drink, because he came to get me. The bar is full of peasants and the smell of schnapps. A few are shouting and banging on the table and singing rude songs. 'Well,' says the peasant, 'what did I tell you?' He points to me, and everyone laughs. They offer me plum brandy and *treyf*. I drink, but I don't touch the meat. One of the goyim says to me, 'If you've put the horse to, and ridden out on your cart on the Sabbath, then surely you can eat unclean meat as well?' They laugh and laugh and they mop their faces. I remain serious. 'The Sabbath—today? There must be some mistake, my friend. Tomorrow is the Sabbath. Whoever comes to Meir Bernstein to make a mug of him, he must be from yesterday. Get the landlord, young man, ask him what day it is, the Sabbath or no?' The landlord, to whom I lent a thousand zlotys, he doesn't want me to come and mortgage his tables and benches and his horses, and he looks at the peasants, and then he looks me in the eye. 'No,' he says, 'today is not the Sabbath, tomorrow, if God wills it, is the Sabbath.' The peasants laugh and shout. Outside, Gallach walks by, the Catholic priest. 'Call him, tell him what's happened, ask him what he says!' Gallach looks in their faces, which are wet and red, the eyes dimmed from booze. He shakes his head. 'If Meir Bernstein has laid hands on the horse's collar and turned the screw on the gate, then Meir is right, it can't be the Sabbath!' "

Perez and Berkowicz have given up, because another man next to Meir Bernstein, who also has shoes and a coat, has died faster, and now they share the inheritance and creep under the canvas. For evening is drawing in, milky white fogs are dotted about on the slopes and over the forest, a swarm of black crows flies up almost noiselessly, the air is damp. Someone has brought along a piece of canvas, the size of a blanket. They spread it out, and under it lie some twenty men, pressed together like herrings. Whoever lies under it can hardly breathe, but at least he's warm. On the first night I lay under it, but tonight I'm not lying under the canvas. All around sit the old and the feeble who don't go under the canvas because they would die there, and who don't lie down but remain seated because they know that the light goes out when you sleep, that you fly away without a sound, like the crows. And they want to stay alive. But why?

I could sleep, but tonight I'm not going under the canvas, because I've taken a decision to flee. I'm going to try it at night, not stupidly, like Chaim Jitzchok. Long after midnight, when the jackboots are asleep on their feet, slumped over the sides of the cars, not moving, that's the right time. The train puffs through the night. I wonder where we are now, there's no light, no little gleam of hope. I carefully go over the plan, my blood-starved brain needs hours to arrive at a clear thought: it must be dark, I say to myself, no snowy fields, only woods and bushes will give me cover. I hunker by the side of the car, freezing, my eyes falling shut. To sleep under the canvas and not be cold seems the greatest happiness in all the world. Why torment myself? To try to flee in this country may be certain death. But no more than staying here with the others, who one after another stretch out. What to do? The men are all dozing or asleep, not one is awake, they are not suffering. Condensation mixed with soot settles on their skin. One of the two sentries, at the front, in the corner of our wagon, is still smoking a cigarette, but he's almost falling asleep over it. I drill my nails into my palms to stay awake. The wooden planking of the cars is creaking and singing, the iron jangles, whines, and moans, it's a bitterly cold night. If I fall asleep, I'll freeze, if I make my break too soon, they'll pick me off with their rifles. I need to stay awake and be patient and endure my thoughts. Meir Bernstein will be dead by now. Perhaps he'll move his lips once more, an angel will fly past his eyes in death. God the Father, whom one may not see, is waving with a palm frond from behind a picket fence, and Meir Bernstein calls out to him, "I'm coming, old man, I'm coming," he calls, "wait just a moment longer, I'm coming. Because life is so sweet!"

"Don't sin," Meir had said to a Christian during the march over the Giant Mountains, who had wanted to make an end and run into the line of fire. "Don't sin. Everything else you may give away, but life itself is not yours to give. Only God may take it from you, and none save only Him."

And now it's time: the train is puffing its way up a hill, the sentries are slumped over the sides like sacks. I pull myself up, slowly, because each movement could wake them. And then I look over the side, see the countryside, flat and snowy, a great expanse of white . . . It's decided, the country doesn't want me. I slump back, I fall on the canvas, beneath which the sleeping bodies stir and kick, and someone curses me. That's the voice of Lederer from Charleroi, the coal miner, he seems to have strength left, the way he hacks at my back through the canvas with his knees and elbows. Or perhaps I'm suffocating him . . . In the morning they'll drag him to the front of the car, where the dead go. They'll put him with Meir Bernstein, and take his shoes off him.

He had come to our camp in the fall of 1942, Meir Bernstein, having lost everything, his fields and his animals, his wife and children and the last of the gold pieces that were sewn into his jacket, which was torn off him. For a long time he kept silent. Only later did he begin to speak. Through his own words, for the duration of two years, he lived his life over again, got everything back—to lose it again, piece by piece. First of all, his beloved daughter. She died on a sunny day, in the middle of summer. She was playing in front of the house when the hay wagon tipped over and crushed her. Meir didn't complain, didn't wail like Job, didn't argue with his god. All he said was, "Recha, my little Recha, she was happy and innocent."

Erich Pechmann, who could make music with his five fingers, interrupted Bernstein. "God takes the happy and the innocent to himself."

Meir Bernstein despised western Jews, and Pechmann was a western Jew; what was he doing blathering about God? "Quiet," Meir Bernstein hissed at him furiously, "don't talk about things you don't understand."

"But look," the other persisted naively, "she died happy, God spared her sufferings like ours . . ."

Meir Bernstein shook his head. "Recha should have lived. She would have accepted suffering with open hands. Living, living is everything, suffering is nothing!"

I remember another conversation, following a day off work, in the darkness of the barracks. Meir Bernstein and Mendel Teichmann had taken it in turn to tell stories, had gotten drunk on words, had evoked the scent that dwells in the narrow lanes on *yontev*, outside the houses of wealthy Jews, drawing the poor, who stand by the door waiting for presents. The aroma of roast veal and fishes, of onions and wine vinegar, raisin cake and oranges. The shining eyes of the little ones, singing and laughing, and the peals of girlish giggles. Then there was a break in the storytelling, and Meir Bernstein's voice suddenly cracked. "Sinner that I was, damned conceited sinner. Thinking I was rich and out of reach of misfortune, for all time. That my blood would triumph in my children and my children's children."

And out of the dark barracks, where the tired men were listening, the voice of Mendel Teichmann: "The curse on us is like the

water of the seventh well. Do you remember the words of the great
Rabbi Loew? 'The seventh well will wash away what you have collected, your golden candelabra, your house, your children. Naked
you will be left, as from your mother's womb. And the honest water
of the seventh well will cleanse you, and you will become transpar-
ent, like a well yourself, made ready for future generations, so that
they will climb from the darkness, with a pure and a clear eye, and
a light heart.' "

I did fall asleep after all, and I didn't freeze. When I awoke, the train
had stopped. The dead lay piled up on the front platform of the car,
as on a heathen altar, one on top of the other, and Meir Bernstein
on top of all. He lay chill and stretched out, his bony face almost
black, mouth and eyes shut.

On another track, not far from us, recruits for the front were
being put on trains. They were very young, not much more than
boys. Horses whinnied, the young soldiers bantered and laughed.
What was it that had dulled their senses so that they were able to
laugh? The morning sky was a bright, poisonous pink. The buildings on the slope were a muddle of shadows. People lived there, ate,
drank, slept in beds. The men in front of me, both living and dead,
ragged as tramps and gypsies—silent, frozen tramps—how miserable was their ignorant suffering.

Slowly the train moved off. The busy streets of the town seemed
somehow stony, empty and dead. People stood around in them fascinated, unable to move. A railway-crossing attendant, a policeman,
a man on a ladder cleaning streetlamps. He looked down in our
direction, his shoulders hunched around his face, a twisted expression on his mouth, as though he were saying, "Peace to your ashes."
Or else, "Go to hell!" It could be either; we weren't to know.

That morning Bertrand Lederer from Charleroi died and
Abram Larbaud from Montpellier, Efraim Bunzel from Prague

died and Samuel Wechsberg from Lodz, and others died in the cars on either side of ours, whose names we never learned. A religious man was praying next to me: "*Shma Yisra'el, Adonai Eloheinu Adonai ehad . . .*" Praised be your name, Eternal One, who has chosen us from among all the peoples . . . His eyes had a dull gleam like copper. There was no longer enough warmth in his body or moisture to make his breath cloud like that of those people in the streets. The train was picking up speed, it clattered over the points, it shook us about, causing the odd man to wake up with a groan. The sky became steel-blue and deep, and only scattered little pink clouds smiled down, like innocent children.

6

KAREL

His close-set little eyes, always looking strained, offended, surprised, a little dismayed, gave him a certain resemblance to a monkey. The only time he used his glasses was for reading and operating. Then, looking calm, concentrated, and merry, he cut open the boils of the sick. A long time ago, he had taken a couple of semesters of medicine, but then, as he said, he had hit the town. His parents, well-off carpet merchants in Lyons, had spoiled him. "I was a boy genius," he said self-mockingly, "a prodigy. Studying was no harder for me than eating cookies. I read a book a night. Passed all my exams with distinction. So smart, it could make you sick. What for would I be a doctor? With my brain, I could do anything that took my fancy."

His father, a little Russian Jew, was a martyr to hemorrhoids and a boggy prostate. He hoped his son would one day save him the expense of doctors' fees and heal him, whereas those leeches of specialists only made things worse. What was a sick Jew good for? A milch cow for the medical profession. But then his father died. His mother went to Tarnopil to stay with her sister, whom she hadn't seen in twenty years. All alone in Lyons, Karel (his real name was Charles, but here in the camp everyone called him Karel) gave up his studies, invited prostitutes into the apartment and a bunch of new friends he barely knew. They stole whatever wasn't nailed down, or else broke it.

"I always had high standards," Karel would quip. "First it was a book a night, now it was a different woman. I discovered women in a big way. I was as ugly as a pickled cucumber, but the little honeys of the rue Mercière went for me all the same. The red-light district in Lyons isn't very big, so before long I was a prince there.

Well, I was throwing money out the window with both hands, as they say. God forbid that a Jew not be able to manage money! Ten Jewish misers couldn't extort as much as a single spendthrift can put other people's way. And do you believe I ever regretted it, you fool," he would ask anyone who happened to be listening. "What did you miserable flea-flickers ever do with your lives? Always crippled with worries and fears that there might be bad times ahead? And now?"

Anyone who took issue with him would get a dose of his sarcasm. He didn't spare even his patients. Mostly they were so shocked by what he said that they kept perfectly still and forgot their pains for a few minutes. Once, a Muselman came to him with a hand as puffed up as a swollen liver sausage. Karel told him to sit down and lay his hand flat on the table. The boil was flush on the wrist, he had to operate immediately. He got out the basin for the pus and the rusty scalpel. There were no anesthetics and nothing to cleanse a wound with, beyond a little potassium permanganate. Karel said calmly, "We'll soon kill that little porker for you." Then he turned angrily to the patients, who were groaning and raving and arguing on bunks round about. "Quiet!" shouted Karel, and added a long string of blasphemies. "Open the window, the stench here is foul enough!"

The new patient had beads of sweat on his brow. Karel sat down serenely opposite him, felt the swelling and, with his alarmed and offended expression, looked into his eyes.

"How old are you, *khaver*?"

"Twenty-one."

"Where are your parents?"

"Gassed."

"How do you know?"

"I was told."

"Any brothers or sisters?"

"A brother and a sister, both in the camp."

Karel prepared his instruments, then he said, "Perhaps they've already been shot or hanged. And you, you're afraid of a little cut with a knife. Keep still!"

The patient held out his hand, and Karel sliced open the swelling with a single cut. A second cut across, and the pus flowed into the bowl. The young man didn't move or make a sound. Now it was all over, it was Karel who had beads of sweat on his forehead. He laid a strip of paper bandaging over the wound. "Whew," he said, "you've got some nerve." For a moment, the patient saw the traces of extreme concentration and pain in Karel's features. But already he was turning to the next one.

Karel found the Jewish songs that were often sung on days off unbearable, because they were so often performed with tearful voices and heavy sighing. It was only the comic songs from the ghetto, which were in the minority and full of disguised bitterness, that he liked. He said, "Sentimentality is a Jewish disease which you have to shake off. The Germans are exterminating us, and they're sentimental as well."

All his activity, his inexhaustible energy, went into masking his feelings. He squirted poison like an adder. And yet he spent sixteen hours a day working with the sick. Fetched water, boiled shirts and cut them in strips, gave a dying man a mouthful of soup, settled differences over a piece of bread, ran through the barracks hunting for a man suspected of carrying typhus or prisoners who couldn't get up in the morning and were already half-frozen. The actual prisoners' physician and Karel's superior, Dr. Levin, a tall handsome man, already tired and resigned, or perhaps grown a little indifferent, was no longer astonished, no longer shook his head at Karel as he had done to begin with. "We don't have any medicines," he had used to say, "what are you running around for, making everyone *meshugge*? Let them die quietly." Now he let Karel get on with it.

He was almost infected by the mania of his assistant. He no longer seemed to be so indifferent in the face of death, he listened with more patience to people's laments, no longer moaned when someone called him out at night.

On one occasion, they brought him Alek. The boy had fallen off some scaffolding, and lay there brokenly. The Kapo brought him in in a wheelbarrow. His limbs hung crookedly over the edge of the barrow. Alek remained alive for another half an hour. Dr. Levin and Karel fussed over him, cut his convict's clothing off his body, gently, carefully washed him, talked to him. Alek breathed heavily and unevenly, made incomprehensible gurgling sounds and kept his eyes stiffly open. We all knew his story: Alek was born in Tunis, had lived in Brazil, had moved with his mother to Paris and Grenoble when she lost her husband, had been to school on three continents, could speak five languages, had married at the age of twenty—and enjoyed the best days of his life in the camp of Rivesaltes at Perpignan, near the Spanish border, wrapped in a blanket with his Nadja. The prisoners lay on the ground in the barracks, or on straw and paper and blankets. Their blanket was their honeymoon suite. They lay there in a silent intimate embrace, respected by all. The honeymoon voyage was to Drancy, and then on to Auschwitz. There they were parted, and it was over.

Karel pleaded with him aloud: "*Khaver*, you know Nadja's on her way to you," he said, "don't worry, she's coming . . ."

"What are you doing, you idiot," cried a sick old man from his bunk. "Why are you lying? It's wicked to lie to a dying man!"

"Am I lying?" Karel retorted coolly. "What makes you so sure I'm not telling the truth?"

"But he can't hear you," wheezed the old man, "he can't hear you anymore!"

Karel spun round, with his astonished expression on his face.

"Why are you shouting like that, and making a fuss? What business is it of yours?"

The old Jew tore at his hair. "You should talk to me, talk to us, he can't hear you."

"You know?"

"I know."

"Quite sure?"

The old man rolled his eyes. The others followed the quarrel, grinned, sniggered.

"What do you mean sure," asked the old man stubbornly. "Nothing's sure in this world."

"In other words, you don't know whether he can hear, or if he's already deaf," said Karel. "Well, I don't know either, and that's why I'm talking to him, so that he doesn't feel all alone, wherever he is now . . ."

Two hours later, another young Jewish boy fell off the same part of the scaffolding. He was dead on the spot. And the Kapo trundled him into the camp in the wheelbarrow too, which was white with plaster dust, spotted with red. We were stunned when we saw it. Was it coincidence? Murder? Someone whose hobby was throwing Jewish boys off the scaffold, and was able to indulge himself? We never knew. No one asked any questions.

We had sunrise and sunset in the camp too. Some days bleed dry like a discarded bunch of narcissi. And then there are glowing, sputtering evenings. Mornings when a sun comes up bloody as out of a battle. I remember one red Sunday morning. The sun hid behind veils of haze that glowed a milky red and then lilac, like the cheeks of our consumptive brothers. It was icy cold, steam clouds vomited out of the doors of the kitchen barracks. We envied the kitchen personnel, striding through the camp gates with their sleeves rolled up to show off their muscular arms, not freezing, back and forth between the kitchens and the supply room, the *Prominenten* of the camp. But there was greasy smoke also from that part of the barracks where the artisans lived, the camp cobbler, the tailor and others. They were frying a cat there, you could smell it a mile away.

I'm talking about a time when Pechmann was still alive, when Chukran was setting the comrades on fire as he did every other Sunday with skillful descriptions of delicious dishes, when Mendel Teichmann was sitting on the foot of his bunk, meditating aloud, and ten Galician Jews were saying *kaddish* in the washroom. The old actor Baer had just recently lost his mind. He was talking wild stuff, gesturing like on stage, and strutting about proudly but somehow brokenly. When one of his old friends spoke to him, he smiled a lofty tragic smile, swayed, didn't understand, and was obviously weakening by the minute. Karel was called. Karel addressed him: "*Khaver*, it's bitterly cold, what are you doing out of doors, have you lost something? You'll catch cold standing here. Go to bed, don't go to work today. If you take it into your head to go walkabout, they'll come for you."

Baer seemed to be standing in the midst of a gathering of councillors and worthies, that's how puffed up he was. "Gentlemen," he said contemptuously, "when I was twenty-five years old, I played King Lear in the Arts Theater in Krakow, you can't expect me to make a fool of myself, and moreover . . ."

Karel could see it was no use talking. He gave a nod to one of the kitchen staff. The fellow picked up Baer in his arms like a big doll and carried him inside. Applause and laughter could be heard from the kitchen barracks. The kitchen boy, an eighteen-year-old giant from Kalisch, swaggering and unimpressed, grinned. Karel tried to wrap Baer in blankets. Baer struggled and wept like a child. He scolded softly to himself, but in powerful oaths. Philistines, without a clue who he was. He ended up crying himself to sleep. Schloime, his nephew, a dirty stupid young man, abjectly devoted to his uncle and terrified that he might die (because every day Baer got a liter of soup on the strength of his reputation, which was the highest accolade the camp elders had to give), and then where would he get a helper from? Ever since Baer had lost his mind he no longer touched his free soup, which he had previously shared with Schloime. Schloime tipped it greedily down his own gullet.

Men were pulled in every day to the wagons, at night and on Sundays too. Wheels had to roll for victory, we could read the writing on the side of the cars in white letters. There were always pipes to be unloaded, concrete parts, wooden beams, planks, and bricks. That morning too they had selected thirty men to do the unloading. The Kapos darted through the barracks and chose: dirty, lousy, and feeble men, but also strong men who didn't enjoy protection from any of the *Prominenten*. No one knew by what criteria the Kapos made their selections. For sure, they lit on people whose faces didn't fit. Anyone who had been selected once for Sunday duty lived in fear, did everything not to attract attention during the week, and tried for all they were worth to ingratiate themselves with the Kapos. But often it was all to no avail. Not to have a day off after fourteen sixteen-hour days was often the end.

When the Kapo got Altschul out of his bunk, he sobbed and acted weak and ill. He was weak and ill, and it wasn't hard for anyone to appear still weaker. And sometimes the Kapo would have mercy. But he needed to present thirty men within ten minutes at the guard post. If he spared one Muselman, that meant punishing another, whom he would have to take instead. In this way, the Kapos soon became immune to feelings. Altschul had to go. We watched the thirty men march off into a light blizzard, while we sat around and hunted lice in the barracks. Altschul's lanky form brought up the rear. The guard gave him a vicious kick that sent him sprawling in the dirt. He didn't get up again. The jackboots strolled up to him, and they would certainly have made him get up in a hurry. But instead his comrades grabbed him and pulled him away.

He was a little middle-class boy from Dortmund, a bloody western Jew. His parents had given him the Germanic name of Kuno.

But nothing had helped, not the blue eyes, the straight blond hair, the tall Nordic form—a Jew was a Jew. He was a good-looking boy, all right, our Kuno Altschul, but not very smart. He failed to pick up the tricks and ruses, the cunning we needed to survive. At work, he quickly burned up his energy, instead of using his eyes and only applying himself when it was really necessary. In turn, he would draw attention to himself through being tired when it was essential to prove one's vigor. He didn't understand that. It caught up with him when he was unloading bricks, he was caught between the buffers as a wagon silently came up behind him. He screamed the entire way as they carried him back to the camp. Karel ran to the camp elder, begged him to ask for morphine from the SS Oberscharführer Wenzel. The elder shook his head. "I know what Wenzel will say. 'What do you think this is, a sanatorium? There's a war on. Morphine is for soldiers, not for Jews.' That's what he'll say."

Karel ran back. Altschul was lying on the wooden table with a crushed pelvis, screaming. All the patients who could so much as crawl left the infirmary. The camp elder, Dr. Levin, and Karel stood by. They should have been able to knock the poor man unconscious, but not even that was possible. For the first time, Karel lost his nerve. In the cubbyhole he slept in with Dr. Levin, one could hear him cursing: "If anyone had come to me back in Lyons and said, 'You dirty Jewish bastard!' I'd have finished my studies, and my eyes would have been opened . . ." Then nothing was heard for a long time, just brief groans of despair. And then the voice of Levin: "All right, *khaver*, and if you'd finished studying, how would that have changed anything today?"

One morning, a couple of hundred prisoners were standing in the yard. Wenzel was reading from a piece of paper, the orderly was writing down names, and the Kapos were combing the barracks, looking for men. But they weren't looking for the sick and the feeble, the Muselmen, as usual when there were offers of "rest and recreation" at Auschwitz (through the chimneys, as everyone knew who no longer believed in fairy tales). The two hundred were needed for a new factory somewhere near Gliwice, where—just think of it!—they would work indoors, in rooms. Everyone who was chosen was jubilant. I snuck out of the sick-barracks and stood in line among the chosen ones. But Wenzel and the elder walked down the lines, grabbed everyone by the scruff and gave them a shaking. The feeble ones sagged at the knees, and were rejected. I wept when I saw them leaving the camp, wept with rage. And Karel—at the very last moment, they got Karel too. He had pulled on a medical orderly's satchel and run along after the unit.

A couple of weeks later, we heard there was an outbreak of spotted typhus in the new camp. We didn't believe it, because they brought Karel back to us, along with some writer called Berger, a political prisoner, whom they still needed. Then Berger came down with spotted typhus too. He was delirious and was shut away in a separate section of the barracks, along with Karel, who was assigned to look after him. The door was nailed shut, and Karel was given what he needed through the window. We were told how in Gliwice they had nailed up the doors of the prisoners' barracks, yes, and the windows too, even though not everyone was infected, not by a long chalk. They were just left to starve. They didn't need any of them, seeing as there was no shortage of manpower from Gross-Rosen and Auschwitz.

One day the writer was dead. Karel remained quarantined for four more weeks. We saw him running back and forth in the room like a caged animal. No one else returned from the other camp. Karel was the only survivor. There was sadness and bitterness in our camp. A father had lost his two sons—and he had been so proud that they both had been taken! There were still cousins, brothers, friends. At night we could hear muffled songs of grief, groaning and complaining in the barracks.

"Did you know my Zikmund?" I heard a Jew asking the man in the next bunk to him. "No, you didn't know my Zikmund, because he was not himself when he came with me to the camp. Because he lost his mind when he saw them killing his mother. A heart like a glass bell, a light crack, and it doesn't ring anymore . . ."

It was dark in the barracks, the only light through the window was from the searchlights mounted on the towers over the barbed wire. Another voice said, "Lord, our King, we call on you from the depths, take us to you!"

Most of the men were sleeping, groaning, snoring. "It cost him his mind," said the old Jew, still talking to his sleeping neighbor, "it cost my Zikmund's mind. And us? How much more will we have to see? Why don't you take away our sense as well, Lord, please, I beg you, take away the yoke and the knowledge from my brow!"

"Because the world is beautiful," I could hear Mendel Teichmann reciting in a soft tender voice, "and the dew wets your tired eyes, which never cease to be astonished at your beauty. O dawn, smile upon our nightmares . . ."

"But when I go back to Chelmno," a Galician Jew lisped in his fever, "what shall I say? How will I look, standing there all alone? The windows will no longer be lit up for Shabbes, with the candles and the children's eyes. When I get back to Chelmno . . ."

"No one will go back to Chelmno," snapped another Galician Jew. "Chelmno is no longer in this world!"

The day Karel came out of quarantine was the day Pechmann died, as already related. Karel acted as though he had never been away. He immediately took charge of the infirmary, ran around, exhausted himself, fetched water, boiled shirts, God knows where he managed to get hold of them, cut them into strips and made bandaging. He sliced open boils—"just like Mamme dividing the

fish on the Sabbath," one of his astonished patients remarked—he
scolded, reviled, poured scorn on everything that moaned and
wept in self-pity. With his hands that gave out strength, he helped
a dying man by holding his head and dribbling water onto his
chapped lips.

I had been visiting Pechmann (I was no longer lying in the sick-
barracks). Pechmann was stretched out on his top bunk, barely
moving anymore. His large eyes burned like coals, he could hardly
speak. Someone owed him for his margarine ration. Jankele from
the fifth barrack, who had been swapping with him for a week,
margarine for bread, because Pechmann could no longer swallow,
his salivary glands had failed, and he was surviving on soup and
margarine. For two successive days Jankele had failed to bring him
the margarine, even though he had already got Pechmann's bread.
His daily ration of margarine, the size of a child's thumb. And I went
to Karel and demanded that he call Jankele and extract the margarine ration from him. But Karel didn't even listen. I couldn't
understand him. I lay in wait for him, forced him to listen to me.
Then Karel shook his head, glanced across at Pechmann who was
lying perfectly still on his bunk, only his eyes moving. Outside the
door, Jankele was dealing, trading the margarine ration that he owed
Pechmann to another invalid who couldn't swallow. "No," said
Karel, "leave Jankele his margarine. Maybe he can use it."

I didn't understand. I hated Karel, I couldn't believe he was capable of such injustice, that he had given up on Pechmann. Just like
that. And now, when, as we heard, the Americans were advancing
and the Red Army all but had Germany in its grip. Then, when I
went to visit Pechmann the next evening, he wasn't there. It was
August 4, 1944. The Allies continued their advance.

But now back to the place I had got to: the beginning of 1945. We
had crossed the Giant Mountains, and had the long journey on the

open cattle cars behind us. The train was chugging up a long slope, through thick forests. Next to the tracks, a road wound in and out. "The road of blood," said one of the comrades in our car, he knew the place. There were long lines of prisoners marching, trucks were pushing their way through the crowds, also cars carrying officers who stared expressionlessly through the misted windows. SS sentries bellowed, from time to time shots were fired. The mountain seemed to ring with a vast industry. The name Buchenwald lodged in our bones like a fever. Of the sixty prisoners in our car, perhaps a dozen or so were still alive. They sat hunkered dully on the bare boards. The jackboots up on the running boards between the cars got ready for arrival, gave youthful shouts, called coarse words to other jackboots on the road, smoked or crammed the rest of their journey rations into their mouths.

Just as we reached the top, the sirens sounded. The sentries leaped off the cars and hid in the forest. The train went into a siding and stopped. Nothing more to be seen: no human being, no uniform. A small station building, various camouflaged barrack buildings. Where was the main camp? There on the slope, on the other side of the peak, surrounded by forest. Then we heard the all-clear. The jangle of the heavy iron bolts on the wagon doors. But not the usual guttural voices gruffing, "All right, all the men out!" Only the metal sliding of locks and bolts. When it came time for our car to be opened, a couple of pale faces peered in, before going on to the next one. Whatever was alive crawled to the opening and dropped down. The snow was too old to break anyone's fall properly, and some who had got that far remained lying on the ground where they were.

Everywhere lay the harvest, in and under the cars, on the tracks, on the roadside ahead. Only a few had the strength to stand up. When they did, they stood in wonder: women, with shopping baskets and pushchairs! A film gone insane. Instead of the main camp with bellowing SS men, instead of the craven, sadistic, noisy Kapos, always intent on promulgating fear and discipline wherever they were—this silence. An eerie small-town idyll. Women emerging from an air-raid shelter, hurrying back to their hearths, their pots and pans, carrying bread, milk bottles, apples, beer. Children, with knitted blue-and-white-striped caps. A sky overhead in forget-me-not blue and white clouds over the tops of the trees, delicate as Brussels lace. The women and children had to go right past our halted train. But they didn't look at the train, didn't see the curious figures tumbling out of the cars (was it a scene they were too familiar with?), crawling along the ground, twisting silently this way and that, trying to get to their feet. Then one young woman fainted. Someone caught hold of her pushchair to keep it from rolling down the hill. No one spoke. The young woman lay on the path. She had seen us. The only one.

And then we saw too: on the edge of the road where the wives and children of the SS men were going shopping were great stacks of railway sleepers, a long row of them, each stack built up of criss-cross layers, four and four and four, to a height of six feet. Only they were dead bodies.

There were women and children on the Ettersberg. Shops that sold meat, bread, and apples. There were houses with beds, carpets, and laid tables. There were radios, glass-fronted cabinets full of knick-knacks, and pictures on the walls. I looked at the train. What were these tumbling figures? Were they human? I saw Karel. He had slung on his medical orderly's bag. His close-set little eyes, which always looked straining, offended, surprised and a little dismayed—they had the coppery luster of death. A smile was welded onto the shrunken face, mocking, a little embarrassed. He dragged himself from one man to the next, as if to ask, Can I help you? But he didn't ask, he no longer had the strength to get out a single sound. When we were marched through the camp gates I no longer saw

him. All over the frozen ground were bodies lying, squatting, jerking. I saw other prisoners wearing thick mittens starting to collect
up the bodies and stack them under the commands of a jackboot,
like railway sleepers, carefully, layer upon layer crosswise, four and
four and four.

7

EZEKIEL — AND THE CITY

A city of a hundred thousand inhabitants. What city? Precinct of Paris? Or Warsaw? Of Brussels? A melting pot of two dozen different nationalities. By the end, the only way even SS officers dare to go in there is with drawn revolver. The Red Army washes over the camps. Auschwitz is liberated. Hundreds of cars loaded with human freight roll toward Buchenwald. Later, whole trains full of corpses will be found somewhere on the tracks outside Dachau and Terezin. The sons of Europe will be found in gullies and forests beside the principal marching routes. Mown down. Assembled on the exercise yard in Buchenwald are the sorry remnants from the camps to the east, evacuated before the arrival of the Red Army. They are led to the pen in front of the effects room. There they are stripped of their rags, deloused and shorn, and for the first time after the long journey given a piece of bread and a plate of soup.

"Give me my pants, murderer!"

"You'll get your pants, with pretty zebra stripes on them and all." Haase, the camp elder Haase, a man with black hair, with thick lips, stands there naked, shaking with cold. Dethroned. Haase, the camp elder from the little camp of Hirschberg in the Giant Mountains, used to go around in patent leather boots, nicely fitting breeches, a sort of uniform tunic, and a white shirt. There were diamonds sewn into the front of his pants (does sir dress to the left or the right?). You wonder how much he managed to extort from the Antwerp jewel merchants. His eyelids are trembling. Prisoners go by either side of him to the counter, where they hand over their bundles of clothes. Then they are dunked in baths of disinfectant, move on under hot showers, submit to the electric clippers. Then they stand there, newly born, squeaky clean and steaming, nothing on their bodies, not so much as a louse. Only camp elder Haase still has his full complement of lice. "My pants!" he screams. "Murderers! Give me back my pants!"

Outside Block 16 in the quarantine camp (the first wooden barracks up on the Ettersberg were built in the thirties), a thousand new arrivals are waiting to be admitted. All are wearing clean pajama suits, all are shorn. Only Haase and a few other Kapos have been allowed to keep their hair—as a sign, as it will transpire. A topsy-turvy organization here, who was to know? They'd have done better biting it off! One of them was hanging upside down by the barracks door. "Are you a Kapo?" a couple of burly fellows ask. "Yes." They spun him round in a steel grip, feet up, his head disappeared . . . Only when we at the back reached the barracks door did it dawn on us. Next to each entrance there was a tiny concrete sink in which to rinse off wooden clogs. My my, they were thorough with their delousing here: bloodsuckers large and small!

Four weeks in quarantine, on a hundred and fifty grams of bread per day. Five men in a rack, four levels high. They are let out just once a day, when the barracks are scrubbed clean. A pedantic SS officer, with a couple of men to back him up, inspects the block. The block elder reports: one thousand one hundred and sixty prisoners, twenty-eight sick, nineteen fatalities! The jackboot writes it down on a piece of paper, baring his horsey teeth. It looks like an attempt to smile, but it's nothing but a reflex. As he takes down his details, correct to the bone, oh, so correct—so many living, so many dead—he stands there in soldierly pose, at ease, chest out, teeth bared. Nothing escapes his trained eye, not a crumb on the damp wooden floor, not a straw on the lousy tubercle-ridden pallets. The living are shivering outside in the icy rain. The dead are in their bunks. The jackboot growls, "Why haven't they been removed? A disgrace!" The block elder says he has several times made his report, but the prisoners at the crematorium had too much to do . . . The men on room duty take the dead and stack them neatly by the door. The pedant grimaces; order in all things.

The scrubbing of the long barracks takes four hours, even five. All that time we stand outside between the blocks in rows. No movement, not a word is permitted. Even so, amidst all the noise of the big camp, the pattering of the rain, the clatter of the columns marching past in their wooden clogs, a few dare to exchange whispers. Next to me a boy, sixteen years old, is crying, with his head on my shoulder. Manasse Rubinstein, inmate of the camp from the age of twelve, beautiful as an angel. That was his salvation, his curse: a Kapo at fourteen! High boots and a rawhide whip. He prefers whipping old men. He whips them dispassionately, with a calm and cold heart. As if he knew any law other than violence. Now he's crying, a boy again. Manasse Rubinstein is washing his stone face and his hands, his bloody hands, with his tears. I see Lubitsch, whom I supposed dead, standing in front of me, and Feinberg the tailor, I see Perez and Berkowicz, familiar figures left and right in the ranks of prisoners. They look at me as I cradle Manasse Rubinstein's head. Do they expect me to push it away with disgust? They don't expect anything, they don't feel anything.

Only one man has pity for Manasse: the magician who took refuge with us in our ranks. On that first day, four men took refuge with us. Buchenwald has its social strata, its hierarchy, its illegals. Three Jehovah's Witnesses and a Frenchman, probably a political, had slipped into quarantine the way one might slip into the catacombs. Will the SS demand their deaths?

The oldest, who carries pages from the Bible concealed about his person and quotes from it incessantly, the oldest, with his magician's face, marked and scored like the ice of a glacier, he doesn't know Manasse Rubinstein's past. He sees a Jewish boy crying, a lost child. He nods affectionately, he wishes he could stroke him. Instead he quotes from Jeremiah: "If ye will still abide in this land, then will I build you, and not pull you down, and I will plant you, and not pluck you up: for I repent me of the evil that I have done unto you. Be not afraid of the king of Babylon, of whom ye are afraid; be not afraid of him, sayeth the Lord: for I am with you to save you, and to deliver you from his hand . . ."*

A commotion in the ranks causes the magician to stop. Jackboots march by. An old Jew standing next to the Jehovah's Witness sinks silently to the ground. Everywhere there are prisoners lying in puddles, no one pays any attention to them. Later, when we are dismissed, they'll be collected up like fallen leaves. Does the magician really believe the words he recites? He carries on, and we all listen in silence: "And I will show mercies unto you, that he may have mercy upon you, and cause you to return to your own land. But if ye say, We will not dwell in this land, neither obey the voice of the Lord your God, saying, No; but we will go into the land of Egypt, where we shall see no war, nor hear the sound of the trumpet, nor have hunger of bread; and there will we dwell; and now therefore hear the word of the Lord, ye remnant of Judah; Thus sayeth the Lord of hosts, the God of Israel: If ye wholly set your faces to enter into Egypt, and go to sojourn there; Then it shall come to pass, that the sword, which ye feared, shall overtake you there in the land of Egypt, and the famine, whereof ye were afraid, shall follow close after you there in Egypt; and there ye shall die."†

*Jeremiah 42:10–11.
†Jeremiah 42:12–16.

*

As we re-entered the barracks, soaked and chilled to the bone, and lay down on our boards, bodies close together, seeking warmth, we heard the call: "Camp elder Haase to the office! Manasse Rubinstein to the office!" Manasse went green and started to shake, as he always did when the call went through the barracks, which happened several times a day. Haase got up from his bed, determined this time to make an end. His comrades held him back. In the box over the door from which the voice came there was a crackling, a whistling, and then we could hear scraps of a conversation in the SS office, from where orders were relayed by loudspeaker all over the camp. Haase had vomited. There was silence in the barracks. All eyes were on Haase and Rubinstein. Two of the earlier Kapos had obeyed the orders right after their arrival—not knowing any better. The SS murdered the Kapos from other camps. They were careful to destroy their helpers once they were no longer needed.

At night, Block 16 trembled, snorted, simmered. The prisoners slept a light, barbarous sleep. But it would be a lie to say there were no little joys in Block 16. Curiosity, wonderment, thirst for knowledge. So I listened to the Jehovah's Witnesses disputing among themselves in the dark of the night. I saw the old man with the magician's face hold a page of the Bible up to his eyes. "He that is far off," he read, "shall die of the pestilence; and he that is near shall fall by the sword; and he that remaineth and is besieged shall die by the famine: thus will I accomplish my fury upon them. Then shall ye know that I am the Lord, when their slain men shall be among their idols round about their altars, upon every high hill, in all the tops of the mountains, and under every green tree, and under every thick oak, the place where they did offer sweet savor to all their idols. So will I stretch out my hand upon them, and make the land desolate, yea, more desolate than the wilderness toward Diblath . . ."*

Whereupon the second Jehovah's Witness read: "Go ye after him through the city, and smite: let not your eye spare, neither have ye pity: Slay utterly old and young, both maids, and little children, and women: but come not near any man upon whom is the mark!"†

The third Jehovah's Witness said: "Is that God's voice, speaking through Ezekiel? Are those not human thoughts? Only man is vengeful and vain, only he would create God for himself in his own image!"

And then Lubitsch. Here in Block 16 in Buchenwald, he no longer quoted Baudelaire. Still erect, though only a shadow of his former self, he sometimes walked between the rows of four-tiered bunks, his eyes full of restlessness and distraction. What was he looking for? I remembered Perpignan, where he had also wandered distractedly through the barracks. He was probably the only man in the whole camp at Perpignan, at the foot of the Pyrenees, to whom it had occurred to found a club. Its members were five or six educated men. I can still see the indulgent or mocking faces of the other prisoners listening to the conversations of the club members. They sat on crates and bundles in a corner of the stifling barracks, and one of them said, "You're wrong, my friend, Madame de Renal was never unhappy, not even when Julien shot at her, even that sent her into ecstasies, if you've read your Stendhal properly! To die by Julien's hand—what more could she hope for! As for comparing her to Madame Bovary, that's ridiculous. Bovary's a dwarfish figure by comparison . . ."

*Ezekiel 6:12–14.
†Ezekiel 9:5–6.

"What I should like to ask you," wheezed another one of the gentlemen, ever at pains not to get any stains on their good suits, "what I should like to ask you"—addressing Lubitsch, who, as they all knew, was a pederast—"is which of the ladies you would have preferred, I mean, for yourself?"

Lubitsch missed the barb, and continued on with the discussion. The conversationalists chortled, and debated the virtues and aptitudes of Mesdames Bovary and de Renal. (They did so in an exquisite French, too.) Another time it was the turn of Balzac to go under the microscope, then they waxed eloquent on the nobility and corruption of Rastignac. They debated the complicated relations between Volkonsky, Rostov, and Trubetskoy in *War and Peace*, raved about Natasha, Anna Karenina, and Kitty, racked their brains to try and remember an entire scene of *Hamlet* without mistakes or omissions, or interpret one of Lear's great soliloquies, only then to fall into a renewed argument as to whether Cousin Pons or Colonel Chabert was the more successful repository of Balzac's own sense of failure and resignation The captive audience in the barracks sometimes complained, or they kept up a bitter silence, full of ominous presentiments, or they mocked those self-infatuated snobs. Outside, long trains were loaded with people being sent to uncertain destinations. Was there really nothing else to talk about? Lubitsch, I am sure, sensed the angry atmosphere, and regretted it, but remained the chief spokesman for the group. A demonstration against barbarism? Who can know.

Even here in Buchenwald his innermost being was still rebelling. Tall, gaunt, mighty bones, sunken cheeks, eyes buried in their sockets, a prominent hooked nose—restless, frittering away precious energies, he mooched about here and there, muttering inaudible spells like a shaman. What were they? Still poetry? Or mathematical formulae or music: last efforts at ordering the chaos that surrounded us?

*

A man I had never seen, but who seemed to occupy part of Block
16 with his powerful voice, would sometimes start declaiming in
French either after rations had been given out or in the middle of
the night. To all of us who were able to understand him, it was clear
that this was an intellectual or artist who had served as a tour guide
in the Louvre while still a student. It sounded a little like this:
"*Mesdames, messieurs*, here you see Géricault's *Raft of the Medusa*.
His masterpiece, if you like. A group of shipwrecked survivors on
a raft, the living and the dying together . . . Géricault's source for
the subject? *Mesdames, messieurs*, Napoleon had just fallen, a world
was going down! See how the artist painted these bodies, glazed
and glistening with brine. Classical forms, through a sheen of
Romanticism. This magical light, a glorification of death, or of life,
if you prefer. And the hope for salvation, in the form of that group
at the back of the painting, those men who have caught sight of a
sail on the horizon. But the question remains, will their ship ever
find them?"

There was a tumult in the barracks. Not that they understood
him, or were provoked by his sarcasm. Hardly anyone was listening
to him. But the strong sonorous voice, and the sheer obstinacy of
this madman, excited their anger. "Shut your dirty gob," one of them
yelled in exasperation, close to tears. A few groaned with pain;
then, with a loud crash, a bunk collapsed. The loudspeaker creaked,
and shrilled with a deafening whistle, as the office passed on
ghostly communications that were not intended for our ears. They
listened, cursed, coughed. It stank in the barracks, miasmas
of pus and rotting flesh. But the madman got to the end of his
monologue:

"You see before you here, *mesdames, messieurs*, the *Massacre at
Chios* by Eugène Delacroix, an atrocity perpetrated by the Turks in

Greece. See the victims lying in the foreground of the painting, waiting for the *coup de grâce*, no complaints in their faces, no fear. Unavoidable, the fate that is approaching them. What was Delacroix's message to us—that we shouldn't care? The Romantic in him called for empathy, feeling, but only in the onlooker, *he* was to feel dread and horror, while the victims themselves . . ."

"*Ta gueule!*" cried a solitary voice in the darkness, shut your mouth! Fresh tumult, shouts, curses, also laughter. Then quiet.

Suddenly the madman begins afresh: "Or *The Lady in Blue*, *mesdames et messieurs*, if you'd kindly follow me, surrender yourselves to these colors, this intoxicating blend of feeling and inner loveliness, *The Lady in Blue* by Jean-Baptiste-Camille Corot . . .

One night, we are woken by a voice. Suddenly, out of malodorous darkness, a song lifted light and magical, an Italian love aria carried by a light tenor. It could only be Antonio! I had come across Antonio before, in the camp at Perpignan, and in the limbo of Drancy. Many awoke and listened spellbound. The tenor was singing exquisitely—perhaps with the last of his strength.

A shout broke in: "Stop it! I can't bear it. Stop it, you're driving me crazy. Stop, stop . . ."

The outburst of that unfortunate ebbed away in a fit of loud, desperate sobbing. Block 16 became deathly quiet, only the rough breathing of many inmates and the sobs of the unknown man—bursting his chest, choking his throat—were audible. Then the singer ended his song. "*Addio amore.*"* It was like poison, like a drug, it drove the blood into our hearts and choked us. A glimpse of paradise. The Jews on the mountain, in the valley below the

*Puccini, *Turandot*, Act II, sc. 1.

promised land of Canaan, behind them the desert where they were
to wander for the next forty years.

In the morning I looked for Antonio. I headed in the direction
from which I had heard the singing in the night. I walked down
the long rows of plank beds, with men lying in them. Something
had sharpened my vision, allowed me to see faces otherwise than
before. Disfigured faces, faces swollen with wounds, with scurf,
with purulent sores, but faces that had still somehow retained some
of their individual character: pride and self-respect, comfort, and a
last shimmer of better days in the past. Someone poked his head
out, the head of a saint, taking in everything with naive curiosity.
Someone hunkered down, his long and shockingly thin limbs
strangely twisted, to pray with closed eyes, rocking back and forth
ecstatically, and pounding with his fists against his chest. There
someone lay quite still, only his hands moving, as though making
signals to an invisible spirit—the convulsions of death. Someone
else was in a waking dream, with a painful smile playing about his
lips. Death was all alone among a great number of men. Some lay
there stiffly, eyes open, anonymous and despised, like deserters:
deserters from a remarkable existence. Then I found Antonio, but
he was no longer living. A little man, with dark skin and dark eyes,
that even as they faded wore a wistful expression of regret, the last
flinching of someone who had seen much that was beautiful. A
Mediterranean type, with sores on his legs and a grotesquely
swollen head on a neck like the stem of a flower.

8

BLUES FOR FIVE FINGERS ON A BOARD

Along with the Jehovah's Witnesses a political had come to us, a Frenchman, as already mentioned, who went by the name of Pepe (certainly his cover name). "Why are we still talking," Pepe scolded us, "what are you moaning about all the time? Because we don't have any rifles? All the time we're talking, comrades are remaining silent in the cellars of the Gestapo. They laugh in the Nazis' faces, knowing full well that their laughter is going to cost them everything, the highest price! The Russian Revolution made the Fascists blind with rage."

His rants were not poetry like the speeches of Mendel Teichmann, they were revolution. The word "revolution" burned on his lips and in his brain. To Pepe the concentration camp was a test he had to pass. Whoever failed was not fit for the revolution. He approached the study of his situation and the people around him with childish zeal: "Tell me about yourself," he would say. Or: "Tell me about Pechmann. What was he like? You keep referring to Pechmann. Was he in the Maquis?" No. "Well, what then," he would mutter crossly. As far as he was concerned, someone who wasn't in the Maquis wasn't worth bothering about.

"Listen to me," I began. "You know what Mendel Teichmann said about Pechmann on the day Pechmann died?"

"I'm not interested," said Pepe, "about your Pechmann and that . . . whatever his name is . . . Cowards, amateurs, what's the point?"

"Listen," I insisted, "your revolution, when it comes to pass, let's say in ten years, all right? What then? Who will live in the world where your revolution has prevailed, only Maquisards?"

Pepe reflected for a while. "Everything will live then," he replied. "Dogs, cats, whatever has lived to see the day!"

"Well then, and now I want to tell you what Mendel Teichmann had to say about Pechmann: that he was an attempt on the part of nature to make a good man. There are a million such attempts. Inexhaustible Nature is patient in its inventions. That's what Mendel Teichmann said."

"Yech," said Pepe, bored, "we can't use good people right now. What we need are heroes, fighters, executioners, knife-grinders, desperadoes."

"You will need all sorts of people," I said, "when the revolution has taken place." I gasped—it wasn't me speaking, it was Mendel Teichmann speaking through me. What had Teichmann done to me? What had Pechmann done to me? And what would Pepe do to me?

"Where did you first come across Pechmann?" Pepe now asked me. He had nibbled.

I said, "In Perpignan, on the Spanish frontier."

"Yech," said Pepe in surprise, "where exactly?"

"In Perpignan, in an old army camp, presumably left over from the First World War," I explained. "In 1942 they collected prisoners and put together long trains for the deportees that finally took them to Auschwitz. At night they had the biggest campfires I ever saw. Why, have you been there?"

"I was born there, but my parents moved to Paris. I can remember the mountains on the horizon, I can almost see them some days, like a purple wall . . ."

"They broke up the old barracks," I went on, "and lit vast fires. The wood was moldy, it was as light as cork, you could crumble it between your fingers almost to dust, and it burned like tinder, the flames were thirty, forty feet and more. The young people danced around them in a ring. They danced a *hora* and sang wild Jewish songs. When someone got tired, he left the ring and lay down somewhere, and someone else took his place. All night, the boys and girls were stamping round and round the fire. A cloud of smoke and dust loomed above the camp like a mountain, underlit by the flames. The prisoners sat and watched in their thousands, and then went to sleep in the barracks where they were eaten alive by sand fleas, were woken up by the singing and chanting, and went back out and stared in the flames."

"What did the guards do?"

"Watched. Same as us, same as the prisoners, stared at the fire and the dancers. One or two of the young men were kept busy collecting wood from the old barracks, to keep the fire going. Glowing embers flew up and scattered in the air like fireworks. The people went gray, their heads were covered with ashes, their faces were scorching. And the chorus sang all night at the top of their voices. They held hands and danced round and round in a circle, like dervishes."

"What did Pechmann do? Did he dance as well?"

"He was one of the wildest dancers."

"What about you?"

"I watched."

"Why?"

"I don't know. I had to see everything. If I'd been in the midst of it, I'd only have seen a part."

"That's not true," said Pepe, "you should have danced too. You don't know what they were feeling. You didn't experience their intoxication. If you weren't in the thick of it, you don't know."

"Maybe you're right," I said. "At any rate, Pechmann was. He fell in love with a Jewish girl called Mariana. She was very beautiful, and he was a good-looking man. I couldn't take my eyes off them. By day they sat exhausted in the lee of a wall somewhere, on the yellow sand, holding each other tight and kissing."

As I talk, at night, in Block 16 in Buchenwald, the pictures return to me and my throat goes dry. Perpignan: a large camp, perhaps twenty thousand souls. A sandy desert, with those gray, rotted bar-racks. In the harsh light of the Mediterranean sun, the termite-rid-dled wood of the barracks has a silverish sheen, like slate or malachite. There are people here from all over France. Men and women, old people and children. The camp is divided up into silos, and the different silos separated by barbed wire. In the morning a group of officers of the Garde Mobile sit down at tables under the white sky and read out names. Whoever's name is called has to go over to Silo 20, and that's where, everyone knows, the transports go from. The French officials don't exert any pressure. The people leave voluntarily. Why do they not put up a fight? Sometimes, when members of a family are called, but other members of the same family not (maybe their turn won't come till the next trans-port, the day after tomorrow), there are cries, laments, even protests. The officials are cool and unmoved. It's an order, they say, the Germans provide us with the complete lists, it's nothing to do with us.

The people stand around, staring at the officers, trembling in case their names are called. Then, once they have been called, they are quiet and they go. That's it.

They come from many European countries. They have emi-grated to France, a country they expected to shelter them, and which is now collaborating with the Germans. Persecution, uncer-tainty, the specter of being transported, have made them soft. They have left fathers behind, mothers, sisters, brothers. Their brothers and sisters may already be "there," in Germany, in Poland, some say in the ghetto, or in Auschwitz, as a few whisper. (It's the first men-tion of Auschwitz, in the south of France.) Where they are, think the Jews, I can be too. When fate has spoken, they adjust to it. Bet-ter an end with horror, than horror without end!

Only a few rebelled: "Why don't you put up a fight? Why do you run meekly to your destruction, like sheep?" Pechmann is among the rebels. He negotiates with the French officials, there are no Germans to be seen. He talks to representatives of the Red Cross, who come to inspect the camp but are unable to do anything. He fights to prevent families being torn apart, tries to stop a mother who's lost her child in the confusion from being sent away. He shouts, swears, pleads, comforts. And at night he dances with Mariana. They hold each other's hands, they stare into each other's eyes, as if they meant to drown.

One day, Mariana's name is called. Pechmann holds her back. "Wait," he says, "don't go, don't step forward, they won't find you here in this crowd! I'll talk to the officials, I'll get you off, I'll try and secure a reprieve, I know influential people here. We'll run away together, to the mountains . . ."

She lays her hand over his mouth and smiles sadly. "No," she says, "let me go, I must."

He knows why. She's told him a hundred times. Her mother is there, and her father, and three brothers. She goes. And from that day forth, Pechmann is no longer rebellious. A week later, when his name is called, he passes quietly through the gate to Silo 20.

There was singing not just round the bonfire. There was a barrack building where young people met up at night. They told stories, sang French, Polish, Yiddish songs. Mostly French citizens, secretly hoping not to be sent away, thinking the mediation of influential friends might secure their release. But one never knew, suddenly when people went missing—were they on transports, or had they actually been released? This is where Antonio sang, where many sang whose names I have forgotten, and Pechmann sang too, and played jazz. Antonio was Italian by birth, grew up in Marseille, fought in Spain, a veteran of the notorious French camps of Saint-Cyprien and Gurs. Antonio sang in Italian and Spanish. The listeners were amazed that there was a man here who could sing so beautifully, in this desert, in the camp at Perpignan. But then why should they be amazed? There were university professors in the camp, surgeons, psychiatrists, actors, writers, and virtuosos. A few may have been released, but all the others were put on transports.

With Mariana's leaving, Pechmann had changed. His gray-blue eyes had a feverish glint. He walked with a slight stoop, as though looking for something in the dust at his feet. In the evenings, he sought company, he beat out a rhythm on a board with his hand. With fingers he played the drums. With his other hand he pinched his nose and mimicked the saxophone. He played the blues. Everyone fell silent when he played. He magicked up an entire band— a one-man band, without instruments. Girls wept silently. Two or three couples danced. Pechmann burned, he was infectious, there was power, sorrow, and poetry in his music. Before long, everyone was humming along, moved to his rhythm, burned with him, in a delirium, unable to stop. Pechmann must have been thinking of Mariana. He couldn't wait to go to where Mariana was, every day he wanted his name to be called. But he was cheerful, and had a soothing answer to every worried question.

"What will happen?" asked an old Polish Jew. "They say they want to wipe us out!"

Pechmann smiled. "Can you work?"

"What do you mean, can I work?" the old man protested. "I'm a painter and decorator! My whole life I've worked, with my own hands. Here, feel, they're hard as stone!"

"Well then," said Pechmann, "they'll find work for you. The Germans are at war, they're sending their own men to the front to fight. But behind the lines, they need people to work."

"But they say they want to kill all the Jews, get rid of us all."

"That's not true," said Pechmann, but he knew he was lying. "If you're fighting a war and you want to win it, you can't afford to kill people who would otherwise work for you. We will work, therefore, and we will survive."

Wherever Pechmann went, he calmed frightened people. He played and he trumpeted: blues for five fingers on a board.

While I was talking, in Block 16, Pepe studied the faces of the men who were lying or squatting nearby, dozing or listening. Pepe kept his eyes open: all these impressions would come in useful some-time, everything was valuable material for his single purpose.

A prisoner came in and fetched Pepe. When he returned, he pulled out a piece of hard, dry bread from under his shirt, broke it in pieces, and gave them out. He wasn't, it seems, completely anonymous; his comrades knew where he was hiding. The Jeho-vah's Witnesses also received supplementary rations from their ille-gal camp organization. After we had ground up the hard bread between our teeth and swallowed it most appreciatively, Pepe said, "Now go on, what happened in Perpignan?"

"It was the time of the wine harvest," I said. "Trucks drove into the camp, selling ripe grapes. Whoever had no money was given some by the Red Cross. The grapes were delicious. Everyone could eat as much as he wanted. The wind blew the smell of the sea into the camp, at other times there were warm waves of scent from the plain: lavender, rosemary, and mint. Sometimes there was a sweet-ish cadaver smell mixed in too. Thousands of rats had made a home for themselves in the deserted barracks. We observed their battles, their campaigns to secure the garbage mounds behind the barracks. In the evenings, many prisoners hung about on the perimeter of the camp, in the hope of getting a breath of fresh air. Sometimes an officer of the Garde Mobile would come along. A tall, impressive-looking individual, with an old-fashioned mustache with turned-up ends. He took off his military cap, rested one foot on a rock, pressed his left fist against his hip, and in his magnificent pose sur-veyed the prisoners. An operetta character, cool to the core, a winning smile, slick and smooth. Of course, many people clustered round him, because he had news for them. He talked about the great theaters of the war, and of the latest transports. While he spoke (and one learned everything and nothing from him), he eyed the young women pretty shamelessly. This time, his eye lit on a girl who was standing by the barbed wire a little to one side. Her mother, a thin and wizened old woman, saw his interest and moved nearer. I saw her making her way through the crowds, to be nearer to the uniform. For a long time she stood at his side, a misty smile on her creased face. The officer, who had several times seen the old woman with her daughter, must have guessed immediately . . . He smiled back at her, even nudged her with his elbow.

"At last, night had fallen, he called everyone nearer. 'I'm in charge of the transport tomorrow,' he drawled with friendly condescension. 'I want to give you some well-intentioned advice: don't make any trouble for us, and don't try and escape from the train. As of today, we have permission to shoot. Anyone attempting to flee will be shot down without warning.' He said this not at all menacingly, but quietly, in a mild and kindly tone of voice.

" 'Excuse me,' a prisoner spoke up sarcastically, 'I don't want to make trouble for you. But you hand us over to the executioner, and you complain that we make trouble for you?'

"The officer shifted a little. 'I'm only carrying out my orders,' he said, a little thrown by the intervention, 'that's my duty. Don't imagine organizing these transports is a pleasure for me. But what can I do about it? Nothing. If I don't run a transport, someone else will do it instead. This is an occupied country. Just think . . . I need to put my family first. I'm sure you understand that.'

"Silence all round. He hadn't expected an effect like that. They stood there as if turned to stone. One could hear the rousing singing of the young prisoners around the campfire, the crackling of the embers in the air, yes, even the whistling of the rats was audible. Now the officer began to feel awkward. The cool silence went on for longer than he could stand. He put his cap back on and made a clumsy movement in the direction of the gates. Once more he turned back to face us. 'What if I refused to carry out my orders, what good would that do? Someone else would come along, and take a harder line. At least I try to be humane, so it's to your advantage . . .'

"As no response was forthcoming, he left. No one said goodbye to him, as they had usually done before. At the gates to the silo he turned back. This time his glance was not for us, but for the girl. He didn't want to miss out on his victim tonight. Everyone was pale after his last words, which told us how things stood. Even the old woman pandering her daughter was hesitating. But then it went through her like a bolt of lightning. She looked round discreetly, and crept off after the officer. That night I watched her with her daughter. She talked long and insistently to the girl. Now flattering her, now scolding her. Her daughter listened to her with large, naive, uncomprehending eyes. In the morning, the place where the two of them had been encamped was empty. Miserable remnants of straw. No one asked where they were. Most probably didn't even remark on their absence, as there were more names called out in the early morning. People got up stiffly from their beds. The dirt, the dust, the stench made them dull. The children were crying. Grandfathers and grandmothers squatted exhaustedly on bundles, among open suitcases, discarded clothes and clay-soiled worn-out shoes left behind by those already deported."

I talked for a long time. All round me everyone was asleep in Block 16, in Buchenwald. Two or three comrades complained, they wanted quiet. Pepe, however, could not get enough. He crept up closer to me, almost pressed his ear to my lips, and asked, "What happened afterwards? Where did you see Pechmann again? Did he find his Mariana?"

"No," I replied in a whisper, "he never saw Mariana again. I saw him in the outcamp at Gross-Rosen near Beuthen. They were building a power plant there."

"But . . . Pechmann," Pepe pressed me, "something's missing . . . you're not telling me something, his character . . . I can't quite imagine him."

"Yes," I said, "probably you're right. He was an average guy, like all of us. There was nothing out of the ordinary about Pechmann. Only . . . how to put it . . . things seemed to get into better perspective when he was around. As if you'd suddenly understood something important about your life."

Pepe shook his head, yawned. My answer hadn't satisfied him. He slid over, down a level, to his bunk.

9

THE SMELL
OF OLD CITIES

Without ever having been to Odessa, to Granada, to Riga, Lemberg, or Kursk, I had somehow encountered the smell of the old cities in the night-black barracks, put together from odd words, melancholy confessions, declarations of love to a place, a street in some outer precinct, a narrow back yard with a pear tree growing in it, a mossy flight of steps, a little house. O destiny of the Jews: when they do settle, they, so widely-traveled, cling with such desperate love to a chance patch of ground. When they lose their home through force of others or fault of their own, they inconsolably carry around the yearning for it wherever they go. Strangers everywhere, they have a pronounced sense of rootedness. At every window, in every doorway they sniff the familiar smell of a little piece of home, even if it is the home of others.

"I was born in Poltava," said Feinberg, "but I lived for forty years in Paris, in the rue des Rosiers, a little Jewish street, just like in Poltava, if you like, or Baranovici. A little lane full of miserable dreamers, who'll scold you if you don't treat them like proper bourgeois! Full of *meshugeners* and thieves, just like all old cities: fantasists, naive businessmen, who, if you're a stranger there, will try and sell you the blue out of the sky and are deeply offended if you question their honesty. They're little *nebbish* scoundrels, not even real scoundrels, because the real ones are already rich and distinguished, and have moved out of the little Jewish lane into a part of town where no one knows them. A lousy lane, the rue des Rosiers, where Moische Kuhn sells fish and Chaim Silberstein sits outside his basement and nails shoes, and the old junk dealer Jitzchok Lemberger bundles old paper. No, he's no longer bundling it, he's no longer selling empty bottles and scrap metal in his back yard. What's that—he passed away in the night? But I only just saw him ...The neighbors are standing outside the house, waving their arms and talking. Only last night they were calling him an old scallywag. Now they're honoring him, and expressing amazement: What, he had a son? A doctor, well really, a professor even. Where? In Philadelphia. Sent the old man fifty dollars a month, nice and regular. He's alive still, and in good health, a fine man! Once he came here to visit, quiet and modest. He wasn't ashamed of his old father, but walked along the street at his side and across the square, with arms linked. He gave money in the synagogue, he paid for new velvet curtains, even though he's no longer of the faith. Well good luck to him, Amen! And then he went away. And the father went back to bundling paper and sorting bottles. Well, what's he to do with himself all day, an old Jew. A dreamer, a fantast. Always with the big speeches telling everyone what's what. *Khokhmes*. He chased his son away long ago, because he wouldn't wear sidelocks and sort bottles. A ne'er-do-well, the father said, and look at him now ...

"A street full of craziness, full of sorrows and tiny joys, where there are still one or two little pale-faced Hasidic boys with sidelocks and black-burning eyes hurrying to synagogue, where women lug home heavy bags full of shopping in time for Shabbes, and the yards are full of steam from the kitchens and the smell of roast goose from over there where a rich man lives, full of the yells of children and the scolding of mothers. The tradesmen stand around in the little square, talking and wheedling and making deals under the open sky, or over a cup of coffee with schnapps. Other men are chatting outside the synagogue, praying, or telling stories with self-important expressions. Foolishnesses. But all the same, what a Jewish quarter like that is capable of producing! It's like a hothouse, stifling, rich humus, wild shoots, but also rare blooms: a mathematician, a doctor, a virtuoso, a poet . . .

"If you walk down a Jewish street, don't be bothered by the superficialities, the noise, the smell, the traders tugging at your sleeve, the pale disturbed faces with wild eyes, the enigmatic imprecations, exaggerations, imaginings—the surface of the sea is wild, but you need to go to the deeps! Hidden away in the Jewish quarter live quiet, modest, hardworking people. We had someone living next door to us for years, few people knew him, he didn't attract any attention. A watchmaker, shy and kind and helpful. He worked ten hours a day, put his savings into a fund for an invention. For many years, he put each free hour he had into his construction. The children were neat and nicely turned out, the wife was a good, quiet woman. One day, they were jubilant, the invention was a success. But the man was mortally ill. I knew a poet once, who never published a line. A quiet, industrious man. He made his living as a nurse in the Jewish hospital. On holidays, he read his poems to the patients, told stories, I've never heard stories like that . . .

"The Jewish street, with its noise and bustle, don't be thrown, don't get tangled up in useless talk about what a bad place the world is, go by, go round the corner and drink a *bromfn* in a bistro in the rue du Roi de Sicile or the rue de Turenne, where you'll find a couple of old trees as well, with benches under them, and by way of background the façade of the Musée Carnavalet. Sit on one little bench and watch the other. It's a mirror. What will it show you? Early in the morning, there'll be a *clochard* lying on it, a tramp. You can watch him get up to begin a new day in that wonderful God-given life of his. He scratches himself a long time, groans, eyes still closed tight, takes a pull from a bottle of red wine under the bench, and rinses his mouth out with wine! Then he draws a deep

breath, stretches, shakes the cold out of his limbs, belches, and pot-
ters off into the city. Tomorrow he'll wake up on a bench somewhere else, in a Metro tunnel, or in the Jardin des Plantes. At ten
o'clock, the local philosophers will come down to the park, the old
guard, a former assistant of the Préfecture, or a retired police
inspector and an old cloth seller from the rue Ferdinand Duval. An
employee of mine, he tells them, with a pompous gesture, imagine,
gentlemen, a *schlemiel*, who's spent half his lifetime selling coarse
linen, dimity, lining silk, thread, trouser buttons, in a word coster-
monger's things, is learning Shakespeare, he knows twenty parts off
by heart, a *meshugener*, he can recite *Hamlet* for you all day long!
While the *grisettes*, the little girls from the nearby tailors' workshops, are rummaging around in the drawers full of ribbons and
shoulder pads, he regales them with "To be or not to be, that is the
question." Or some completely inappropriate passage from *As You
Like It*. And what happened? You won't believe it: thirty-nine years
old, not a hair left on his head, a wife and four little ones, he goes
along and auditions, speaks the parts like a stripling of seventeen.
In the Théâtre des Gobelins, in front of the director. And yesterday
I saw his name on a billboard, like a great famous star actor. He's
made it, he's become a comedian, makes a whole city laugh, that
sad figure, a Jew, a nobody, if you'd seen him. Well . . . so what do
you say now?

"But to get back to the bench. The philosophers have been
relieved by the workmen from a nearby building site, who have
their lunch here, passing around a bottle of wine and cutting up
their bread and meat, every morsel nicely bite-sized, all done with
care and enjoyment. Then along come the young mothers with
their infants, pretty young women, they sit and knit and sun themselves, their infants scramble over the rails, the policeman wags a
good-humored finger at them and makes sure nothing happens to
them. Then in the evening, courting couples sit on the bench and
cuddle. One couple next to another, and sometimes an old geezer

in between, who doesn't see and doesn't look, doesn't bother the couples, just sits and reads his newspaper in the fading light. It might be cold and rainy, but the couples won't be put off. They will sit there till the clock strikes ten, and then the girls will get a little nervous. They get up, and then along comes a *clochard*, lies down on the bench, stows his half-empty bottle of wine underneath him, has a good scratch, and so ends the day, his big, solitary, God-given day.

"I sat on that bench too, it was 1917, the war wasn't yet over, and I wasn't a grown man, I didn't have a beard, my locks made me look older, but my girl loved me anyway, just the way I was. And now I sit on the bench in the evenings, opposite the Musée Carnavalet, and who's kissing and cuddling with her young man? My daughter Germaine! For a while I watch her in bewilderment. Then I creep away. But Germaine sees me, she comes running after me, red face, eyes full of tears: 'Papa, are you spying on me?'

"She trembles with shame and rage. I stroke her cheeks awkwardly. 'No, my darling, I'm not a spy. I was here by chance . . . Remember, I used to come and sit here with your mother. But her father knew, and my mother knew who we were with, there were no secrets in those days in families.'

"And then she cries and stands in front of me, and stares at me like a stranger. And I see: my own daughter knows nothing about me. And what do I know about my daughter?

"But when I get back," says Feinberg, in Block 16, at night, "if I should be spared to see the ground-floor apartment in the rue des Rosiers again in my life, I will just stand and listen, and the walls will speak to me: 'This is where you lived,' they will say, 'this is where you brought up your children, where are they now, did you look after them properly?' And I will reply, 'I believed, I put my trust in God. I was happy,' I will say. 'Every day I was happy. I had my worries, and I quarreled sometimes with my family, with my wife, with my children, and I cursed, and I committed sins of every kind, I lied, I told thousands of little lies, that was my life. But still I was happy, they were my best years, with my children, with my wife, all of us together . . .' But the walls will demand an accounting, and they will ask, 'Here you sat, and frittered away your time. You were a dreamer. You daydreamed. You knew nothing. And what happened, where are they now?' 'I don't know,' I will say. And then I will cry. But the walls will be implacable with me: 'You are crying now, because you have suffered misfortune. But did you cry then? And yet the world was full of misery. Did you not see it?'

"I will cry, and not understand. One can understand the sorrows of others, one can find words of comfort for others, even those who have lost everything. One's own sorrows one cannot understand. Nor find comfort or advice for. And the people who offer advice, because they don't know and haven't suffered—you should flee from them. You should run away and hide. Speak to the walls. Only they know. But because they know, they will remain silent."

10

WHAT DOES THE FOREST MAKE YOU THINK OF?

This is the story of Tadeusz Moll. Cold and hunger and a powerful army of tubercles and typhus germs had knocked great holes in our numbers. But every day new transports came up the Ettersberg, up the road of blood. Humans came and went. The now uncertain hand of the executioner no longer knew its business. Like beasts to the slaughter they drove the prisoners out to the assembly point, and loaded them onto trucks and trains.

I don't remember anymore how I came to be on one of the transports. All at once I heard the singing of rails under me again, and the rhythmic clatter of iron wheels. No one knew where we were going. At any rate, it wasn't far, the land was being squeezed between the first front and the second front, Allied tanks were advancing from both sides. The train stopped somewhere in open country, and then we marched through the dense silence of the Thuringian forest. A remarkable camp under tall fir trees took us in. No barracks this time. Shallow bunkers in the ground, into which we descended, like Odysseus into Hades. Bunk beds stacked all round the damp walls. There were men lying there already, the few survivors from a transport that had got there a couple of hours ahead of ours. From the half-dark of a corner into which I was facing, I beheld the flickering eyes of a boy.

"Where have you come from?" he asks.

"Buchenwald. And where you?"

"Auschwitz. I was working in the gas chambers . . ."

He has little time, he has to take the first listener, a father, or stand-in father. He trembles as he talks, it chokes him like vomit, in spasms. I am terribly tired, my eyes are falling shut, my consciousness is flickering like a lamp on the last drop of oil. I see a boy I must listen to. Things we had often heard and never properly taken in, things we thought were exaggeration, and that someone was now telling me he had personally seen (for a long time to come, I will have the feeling that my diseased imagination has played a trick on me, some Homeric jest): they got undressed, hung their clothes neatly on numbered hooks, and then went in, to bathe, as they were told. Behind them the iron gates were shut. The gas was switched on . . .

"Sometimes we had several transports a day," stammered the boy, "we could hardly get through it. When we opened the chambers, the bodies pressed against the doors tumbled out, knotted together, wet with tears and blood. We carried them in wheelbarrows to the ovens. And we knew: one day it would be us going through the chimneys."

Tadeusz Moll was the name of the boy from Auschwitz, and Petrov was another man who comes into the story, a Red Army man. The former well-grown, contemplative, pale. The other had a foot injury, which he had to keep secret—if you wind up in the hospital here you'll never get out. Tadeusz Moll, pain made him tough and silent, it was etched into his face like a mask of wood. In spite of his torments, in spite of his horrible rags, his dirt and scurf, he couldn't quite keep the Sunday child out of his demeanor. He was a healthy and attractive specimen, there was lightness in his blood, a cunning twinkle in his narrow eyes, a bright friendly smile on his strong mouth. (That very first morning, I'd given him a coat, a long blue army coat without sleeves that I'd organized, and didn't need; he was moved to tears, and remained devoted to me.)

Tadeusz Moll's mother was a pianist, his father a lawyer. Three days after the Germans had marched into Lodz, they picked up his father. Already waiting in the car outside the door was the elite of the street: a couple of secondary schoolmasters, an old retired professor, a dentist, a newspaper editor . . . When Moll talked, he tucked his head between his shoulders, and his face creased up. A child, an old man, Moll was somehow both. In spite of everything he had been through (not long after they'd picked up his father, shots rang out in the park), one could tell he was a pampered boy from a good family. His mother had idolized him. ("Tadeusz, don't run like that, you'll sweat and catch a chill! Tadeusz, my gold, take your time eating, put your book away and sit up straight!")

Already at thirteen, Tadeusz was a little gentleman. He looked down on people in the street. His papa was a good lawyer. Papa was famous! (Shortly after the gunshots in the park, Mama became rather strange, she didn't cry, she was just not there anymore. Or, she had always been strange, and now she took refuge in madness.)

"Where did they pick you out . . . Did you work in the gas chamber?"

Tadeusz Moll scratches his forehead, his rough, wrinkled forehead that gives him such a strangely vexed appearance. "I don't know," he says, "it was in the big yard where they were all standing and waiting. Mama was talking, odd stuff I didn't understand. A couple of men came up, prisoners. They looked at me and said, 'Come and shovel coal with us, you can have a bath later.' They stood me by an oven. It took me a while to realize what sort of oven." ("Swing that spade, swing that spade, faster!" ordered the guard, and then he laughed. "Do you know what that stench is, sonny boy, it's pure Jew fat!")

Tadeusz's hands were soon bloodied from work. He got used to it. And how did he get out of there? He's not able to say that either. He got sick. Usually when someone got sick, they were fed to the gas. But he didn't get put in the gas chamber. The two men smuggled him out with the bundles of clothes from the dead people.

"Who were they, people you knew from Lodz?"

"No idea."

"Did they come on the transport here with you?"

"Haven't seen them. I think they're all dead."

The first morning in Crawinkel, we saw there were Russians, Jews, French, and Poles in the bunker. In twos or threes they pressed their rigid bodies together under a blanket, to get some warmth. Tadeusz Moll, Petrov the Red Army man, and I smiled at each other as we woke up. At four in the morning they chased us out into the cold. Steel stars blinked at us from behind shreds of cloud, the wind ruffled the firs. Kapos hustled us through the bunkers to the gate: "Faster, this way, you idiots, get in line, count down, and get a move on!" The scrape of thousands of wooden clogs, shrill whistles, brutal cries somewhere in the forest. We heard no one complain. Whoever couldn't go on anymore just dropped. One word was handed on from rank to rank: this is hell, *dos Gehennem, ç'est l'enfer!*

Crawinkel was the name of the place near the camp. (Did Goethe not mention some idyllic Krähwinkel somewhere in his oeuvre?) The camp did not offer that practical amenity called a gas chamber. Under the tall firs, bodies were turned to ashes in huge pyres. Swathes of toxic smoke hung sluggishly about the tree roots, and covered the tangle of dead bodies like blobs of cotton wool. At the camp entrance where the prisoners assembled, and were counted and assigned duties, a band played notorious ballads: "O Donna Klara" or "Wiener Blut."* On a stage ten feet up from ground level, musicians, prisoners of course, scraped and tooted and banged on their instruments. The allocation of tasks took two hours. Kapos and jackboots strode along the ranks of prisoners, grabbed each one by the chest and gave him a push or a shake.

*Popular tunes by Strauss and Offenbach. "Wiener Blut," in English, is "Vienna Blood."

Whoever collapsed didn't have to work, but he got no bread either. Whoever got no bread was dead the next day. And each time a work gang headed out, they played us out: *"Muss I'denn, muss I'denn zum Städtele hinaus."** The jackboots barked, "Two three four five, two three four five, get a move on, you shitbags, or I'll kick your asses!"

The apex of the forest echoed, the tips of the firs swayed transfigured. As we filed past the stage, we saw, tied to a pole underneath it, a young man. A strikingly well-formed boy with broad shoulders and long, slightly curving thighs of steel. He was dressed only in a thin convict's uniform, without a coat. With his head lowered, he watched us on our way. In his stone face there was a wild and stern expression that none of us, at that first sight of him, understood. We didn't yet know what was about to happen to him.

Outside, a little factory railway awaited us. A dapper little locomotive on narrrow, damaged rails, setting up a jingling as of cowbells and shaking up some hundred frozen bodies, almost breaking their bones. The prisoners stamped and roared in the icy wind, beat their bodies, swore and yelled. The sound of the clattering cars, and then the echo of the walls of the gorge swallowed our noise, turning everything into a crazy symphony. What were they looking for in the deep defiles near Arnstadt? We drilled holes into the chalk, loaded rocks onto freight cars, dragged concrete tubes and iron props through the deep forest.

Do you remember the forest of Vincennes? And the hot wind in the low shrub woods of Avignon and Orange? The metallic rustle of old burdocks, explosions of lavender and thyme. Have you still enough juice in your brain to picture this: the summer of 1941, after the first few months' internment in the forest of Mayenne?

*"Must I, must I leave the shtetl, whilst you, my darling, stay behind."

You rolled around on the forest floor when you were allowed to leave the camp, remember? With your hands you pulled up moss and earth, you rubbed your face on the good dusty trunks of thousand-year-old beech trees, as one might rub one's face on a beloved's breasts. And later on, that night near Toulouse, in a tractor barn: traitor moon, someone saw you. The face of a young woman through the crack of light at the door, her soft call: *Qui est-ce . . . ?* Who was she waiting for, her brother the Maquisard? Then she sees you, and she looks you fearlessly in the eye. She goes. You think she's gone to fetch the men. But she comes back with a blanket, a warm blanket that smells of horses, half a bottle of wine, and bread.

Or the flight to the Swiss frontier, you had already covered twenty-five miles through forests and over mountains. And now a light at the edge of a clearing. Your thirst is tormenting. The light from the inn draws you inside. I walk in, ask for a drink though I've got no money. The landlord doesn't ask me for money, doesn't ask, who are you, where have you come from? He leads me out across the yard. Now, I think, he's throwing me out. Leave, he will say, get lost, I can't do anything for you. But he opens a door. He opens the door to his own quarters. His wife looks me in the face, and she understands. They don't ask, they don't demand any explanation, they see and they guess, and it's enough. You are given something to eat. They sit respectfully by. Make up a bed for you. Watch over your sleep. At dawn they wake you. When you vanish into the forest, your pockets are full of precious things: bread, meat, sweet grapes. Your hands are still wet with their tears. They begged your forgiveness for the injustice that is being done to you.

Every morning we went to the gully outside Arnstadt, where we unloaded sacks of cement or dragged concrete tubing up the mountainside. All over the hilltops, along the edge of the gully, ver-

tical air shafts are being drilled into the rock. An army of slaves rip-
ping deep holes in the flank of the mountain, to what end? Why
the gigantic exertion? The war was lost, any child could see that.
The fronts were clamping together, the air shook with incessant
bombardments. They drove us on like crazy to work faster and
faster, as if there was something they could do. Subterranean factories for missiles? They didn't need them anymore. Even the ack-ack
gunners had stopped dobbing their little white powder puffs of
clouds into the sky. Glittering in the sun, airplanes skimmed
unmolested down the valley, drew dawdling little circles, dropped
a bomb or two on a station, just for the hell of it. Carefully they
dropped their little bangers into the valley so as not to hit any of
us prisoners. Those were our little breaks—when the air-raid
alarms went off, or when they were dynamiting holes in the rock.
Then the jackboots would scuttle off, and the prisoners had half an
hour to themselves, began to talk and gesture, time enough for
their hearts to lighten a little.

Five or six men get together in a sunny spot. Petrov forgets his
pain, and lays an imaginary table. Clumping here and there with his
stiff leg, miming the officious expression of a waiter, he ushers the
guests into his restaurant. Tadeusz Moll joins in right away. He pro-
duces the man of the world, the cosmopolite pampered wherever
he goes, he's good at that. "I'd like caviar with white bread and but-
ter, and a white Bordeaux!" The waiter nods at each order from the
guest, guaranteeing that everything is available and of the expected
quality. Then he rolls his eyes with delight at the gentleman's
exquisite taste. The spectators are helpless with laughter. The waiter
serves, sweats, brings imaginary steaming dishes which he passes
around and uncovers for the discriminating nostrils to sniff at.
Tadeusz Moll eats, drinks, dabs his lips, his face, his neck, stuffs the
food down his gullet with wild comedy.

I wonder at the inexhaustible resources in such a young person. How could a sixteen-year-old survive the gas chambers without being damaged? Tadeusz caught my eye. Later he came up to me. To cheer me up, he played another scene, in Yiddish: *"Oy, a tepele kave, oy, a glezl bromfn, oy, hob ikh gekholemt a zisn troym. Oy, hob ikh gemakht a shmaytz op di noz, a fargeign!"** He wipes his mouth appreciatively, rolls his eyes with a blissful expression. Then, with no connection, he asks me, "Have you read about the wandering of the soul through the seven skies? You don't know anything about the streams of light and fire and water before the sixth heaven! And the angels call to you: 'Unworthy man, can't you see with your own eyes? Are you one of the children who kissed the Golden Calf, unworthy of seeing the king in his splendor?' "

He stands there in silence for a while, looking serious, introspective. The men all stand there silently. The station building is in flames. A few uniforms start crawling out of the shelters. In a moment they'll start yelling at us again, and making us work. But the sun shines, the sky is blue. Tadeusz Moll blinks at me. "The body suffers, the soul soldiers on. Comfort her, give her a kind word from time to time. When the body suffers, the soul should laugh! That's what Baal-Shem taught us."

We could work out what it meant: five more minutes' break. We wished we could embrace them, the bombers. Their sky-writing spelled victory: sit tight, children, life is beautiful! The prisoners stood fearlessly under the open sky where already the Allies were unchallenged. They talked, they warmed themselves with their words and with the noise of the front. But there were also days when the front went silent. Then the inner fire would die down, our lips freeze, everything listened quietly and waited in apprehension.

---

*"Oy, a cup of coffee, oy, a glass of schnapps, oy, did I have a sweet dream. Oy, how I blew my nose, a pleasure!"

*

Petrov didn't moan, but his ravaged face was white with pain. Every upsurge of courage or exuberance was dearly paid for. After each session in the sun, his leg swelled horribly. He would be left hanging onto the car, shuffling along after it into the mine-shaft and out again, because that was the only way he had of disguising his limp. He was always able to find two or three Russian comrades who were willing to take over his part of the work. They would give him cover, one on each side. If a guard or a Kapo came along, they would start yelling and pushing each other to work faster, and push the car so that it struck sparks. Not one glance was to fall on their sick comrade. If anyone happened to notice his swollen leg, that could only mean a bullet for him.

Another time, as once again a couple of British reconnaissance planes swooped past and our guards had disappeared like rats into their holes, Petrov called me over, produced a couple of carrots from his pocket that he must have picked up going after some farmer's cart, scraped them clean with his knife, and shared his precious find with me. We crunched them up with delight, and smiled at each other. We weren't able to converse much, but the difficulty gave a universal character to such communication as we did have. He would fire off a string of fierce oaths, and then say, "Tomorrow Nazis kaputt! We go home!" And I asked him, "Do you have a wife and family?"

He laughed, held his hand three times at different levels between knee and chest, and said the names. In his narrow eyes was a lust for life. He's as strong as a bear, Petrov, I thought. I could picture him striding through the streets of his little Ukrainian town, with the supple-kneed walk of an experienced rider, a little scorn in the corners of his eyes, and appetite quivering round his slightly upturned mouth: appetite for everything, food, drink, laughter, love. His face was as changeable as a sky in March. With barely detectable movements of his mouth, eyes, nose, he could really say everything. When he laid his hand silently on my shoulder sometimes, it needed no words.

Tadeusz Moll and Petrov are together pushing freight cars, the day is gray and long. The stones are no lighter when it's Moll and Petrov doing the pushing. The comrades see that something must be done. Chukran comes into my head, there was someone who had a solution for every problem. We organize several caps, and then I take Moll and Petrov to the latrine. There's a lot of traffic there. God knows there's nowhere else the men can go, to have a little breather every so often! The guard knows it too. Every ten minutes the guard walks by the latrine. He barks and swings his rifle butt. Better not to take any risks, think the men. A blow with a rifle butt, in this place . . . A couple of unfortunates were sent sprawling into the ditch. That's why everyone hops away at the guard's approach. The guard curses at them from a distance. Why wouldn't he curse, the way they look. He's had it dinned into him, anyway, that they're not human beings. They'd squat there all day if you let them. The guard is sick with nausea and contempt. The later in the day it is, the more irritated his curses, the harder his blows.

"You just sit here till we come for you," I say to Tadeusz. To Petrov I pass on Chukran's nugget of wisdom: "The trick is to pluck out the Cyclops's eye, but without him noticing! Each time the guard comes, you have to be a different person, someone he hasn't seen there yet. Turn your cap round, put on a different one, don't squat in one place, pull faces, change your posture, be upright, then slump again. If the guard sees through your act, then good-night. And keep an eye out for Tadeusz, it's dangerous if he goes to sleep."

Tadeusz Moll is young, he's never been in love, he has no one waiting for him. He doesn't have the cunning to keep himself alive.

But is it not possible he has the wisdom of his forefathers? When I go to the latrine after a couple of hours to check up on them, they're squatting side by side on the pole, chattering away. The guard's just been and gone, now they've got a few minutes' respite. Moll talks Russian with Petrov. He can speak Polish, Yiddish, Hebrew, Russian, French, and German. ("Mama wanted me to go into business, like her brother in Paris. A cosmopolitan, equally at home in Paris as in Lodz or Warsaw. Papa reckoned I was a born lawyer. I learned a bit of everything, but nothing really. What I liked reading best were the old writings, Maimonides, the books of Rabbi Israel Baal-Shem. Grandfather was a Hasid, who taught me to read and sing . . .") When I went back after another two hours, it wasn't Moll but Petrov who had gone to sleep. I let him doze on a while, the guard was nowhere in sight. I could hear Moll reciting sentences in Hebrew. Leaning way forward on the pole, his head sunk between his shoulders, eyes shut, Tadeusz Moll was reeling off sentences:

"God took me out of the midst of the people of the Flood and bore me on wings of wind to the highest Heaven and brought me to the great palaces at the top of the seventh heaven Araboth, place of the throne of Shekhinah and the Merkabah, the hosts of anger and the armies of rage, the Schi'anim of fire, the cherubim of torches, the Ofannim of fiery coals, the servants of the flames and the seraphim of lightning, and he set me to serve the throne every day . . ."

At this point an old Jew interrupted him from the far end of the latrine pole (between them squatted other men, straining or groaning or talking to themselves). "No," the old man said severely, "the words are not 'to serve the throne every day,' but 'to attend the throne.' "

Tadeusz showed no emotion on his pale face. He thought for a second or two. "No," he replied, "it's what I said it was: 'and he set me to serve the throne every day.' "

The old man shook his head in astonishment. "I only meant to test how well you knew it. How old are you, *khaver*?"

"Seventeen."

"You are very learned for one of your age. But you are arrogant, my son. Arrogance leads you to look down on the ignorant. But God is in the ignorant as much as in the lettered!"

I had dropped my guard: at that moment the sentry appeared in the doorway, he hadn't alerted us as usual with his curses, but snuck up on us silently. He picked up a rock and slung it furiously at Moll, who ducked and let it crash against the wooden partition. Then he got up, did up his pants and stomped stiff-legged, on numb feet, but erect, past the guard. The soldier had puffed himself up, his face was purple. He had drawn breath for one of his terrifying tirades. But he remained silent. He stared in his rigid pose at the Jewish boy as he climbed, none too quickly and with not a sign of fear, up the slope, to where the freight cars came out of the mountain to be emptied. The cars scraped and squealed on their terrible rails, the drivers barked, the air trembled with noise. The guard seemed not to notice as a dozen other occupants of the latrine whisked past him. Even Petrov hobbled quickly past.

I have often thought about this scene in later years. Tadeusz had a guardian angel, no question. The story of the two unknown men who twice saved him from death in the gas chambers had something inexplicable about it, but it was not a lie. Or was the explanation quite simply his baffling stoical-naive attitude? And was such an attitude the result of absentmindedness and awkwardness— was Tadeusz clueless in the face of danger, or did he despise it? Did he lack the cunning with which to survive, or was his calm in fact a sign of higher cunning, developed over hundreds of years of persecution? In his beardless, still not fully formed features there was meekness and a note, striking in one of his years, of irony. The guard must have heard a little of the conversation, though of course

without understanding any of it. And his disgust at these alien people, who were capable of spending hour after hour squatting on the
latrine and conducting learned disputes at the same time, that disgust had been supplanted by surprise. Or had he by some miracle
felt disgusted with himself?

That evening, as we swung into the square in front of the office,
to the jolly rhythm of the band (*"Wir sind vom K. und K. Infan-
terieregiment"*), to be counted, searched, and humiliated, we saw: the
lad on the post underneath the band was not alone. There were six
posts, and three of them were now tenanted. Very young men,
milksops, mother's boys. As with the first, their caps and coats had
been taken off them, and they stood there shivering. Or rather, we
couldn't see whether they were shivering, what they were going
through. On their faces lay that stiff spectral earnestness of certain
death, an expression far more gruesome than the expression of
death itself. At last we heard what this exhibition of prisoners
under the bandstand was about. Comrades told us, the ones who
had seen it before: "Just wait," they whispered, "see how many posts
are still unoccupied?"

We were not frightened. Each of us had witnessed various daz-
zling scenes of the great *son et lumière* of terror that the officials of
dictatorship liked to put on for themselves. Besides, we were each
of us preoccupied with our own piecemeal execution, we could
hardly stay upright with fatigue, we were greedy for our bunks, for
warmth and for a couple of hours of sleep. Even the sight of the
living Satan in all his pomp with a great retinue, against the background of hell, where men were simmered in great pans, even that
would not have fazed any of us. It was the hour of sleep. We had a
right to sleep! A bitter brief and sweet night lay ahead of us, filled
with dull delirious visions of food, drink, and a sight of a beloved
face. Once we had drunk our bowls of stinking beet soup, we
threw ourselves down on the boards and fell into a trance. A

bunker like ours full of prisoners must dream up a whole universe! It was a cauldron of helpless desires, creaking like a ship as it takes in water and sinks. Only a few still had the strength to remain awake and converse.

Tadeusz, half asleep, was murmuring something to himself. When the three of us were pressed together under one blanket, a blanket stiff with filth, dried blood, and pus, Petrov and I and Tadeusz between us, we could hear a rushing murmur in our ears: a mechanism, a *perpetuum mobile*, that ran on nothing but life itself and was trying to prevent its own dissolution. At that time, Tadeusz Moll was in a dangerous condition, torn between the desire to live and an ever-increasing yearning for peace. To throw in the towel! To give up and let yourself drop! At that stage, everyone developed a little array of reflexes: one man moved his fingers, his toes, his shoulders; another would nod his head, blink his eyes or move his lips, pray, whisper names or some secret charm. When one's will broke and the reflex snapped, the struggle was over. The man then wanted only to die. And there was nothing easier than that.

In the black solitude of the bunker, Tadeusz Moll was murmuring: "His servants sing to him and confess the power of his miracles, as Lord of Lords, surrounded by thrones, ringed with the peoples of the lords of glory. With a shimmer he wraps the heavens, and his splendor shines down from the heights. Abysses flicker in his mouth, and firmaments sparkle forth from his form . . . But Mama," he interrupted himself in a tenderly mocking voice, "how should I greet the king without bowing? What use to me is my blind pride now . . ."

Roused from my sleep, I eyed him curiously. There was an expression of peace on his childish mouth. He was fantasizing with half-open eyelids, through which tears were oozing. But his whole countenance was in the form of a question, an unanswerable sarcastic question.

*

What does "forest" make you think of, sleeper, you . . . The aroma
of a forest, the sight of a forest, peace in the deep woods, the
rustling of the crowns, the majestic nodding of treetops in the wind
. . . For all time the smell of forest for me will be mingled with the
smell of burning and the image of toxic white puffs of smoke on
the naked bodies of the dead of Crawinkel. But also the memory
of warm afternoons of childhood at the foot of the Kahlenberg in
Vienna, tired and drunk with color and light. The buzzing of wasps
in the tall grasses, the angry drone of horseflies on their quick
flight, their escapades around some tiny disintegrating corpse, half-
buried under ferns. The metallic glitter of their wings and cara-
paces, lulling hum of crickets, and in the distance, also productive
of a pleasant drowsiness, a scrap of conversation under the burning
sun, the laughter of maids and mowers in the fields, a stifled gasp
of pleasure. The world is still at peace. Above the steaming earth is
a profound harmony. But also the memory and the taste of your
bitten lips, the kisses of that girl in Saint-Nazaire, who died shortly
afterwards under the Germans' bombs . . .

Sleeper, do you hear me? The world no more at peace. But I—
I will live for ever. I will be happy. I will be drunk with pleasure
and love. I will be strong and prevail. The aspect of the forest will
never be unmixed for me. Forest, peaceful silent machinery, storing
rainfall and sipping from streams; turning life to rot and rot to life;
plenitude and emptiness; microscopic life and eternity in a dew-
drop, you will never make me forget this picture: a stage in the
middle of the Thuringian forest, set on six thrusting young trees,
musicians on it, droning, scraping, banging, and underneath the
young men, the attractive sons of anxious mothers, young know-
it-alls, light-footed scramblers over wall and fence, toying with
danger, opponents of a hierarchy of deadly laws, barbed wire,

watchtowers and trenches, testers of God—and Tadeusz Moll among them! (The gibbets too, the broad gibbets of good stout oak, on the exercise yard, a rectangle cut out of the green fir wood of Crawinkel, the gibbets also had six hooks. What morbid joker thought that one up? Just wait, the comrades had whispered, until they're all taken. How many posts does the stage have?)

The day had begun quite well. It was no longer so intensely cold, a diseased copper-colored sun came peeping through the gray scraps of clouds. There was a different sentry on guard at the latrine. So again we were able to send Petrov and Moll into exile. Petrov's leg was less swollen, but he had a temperature and needed rest. It was certain that one of them would fall asleep, and that was risky. We organized our roster. Every hour a comrade was to look in on them. But then it wasn't possible to go to the latrine whenever one wanted to. The times when someone was allowed to go were determined by the guard at the rock pile.

Tadeusz made a particularly cheerful impression that morning. But it was a confused, almost drunken cheerfulness, which made me suspicious. By ten in the morning, he had disappeared. We looked for him all over but could find him nowhere, and the more time passed, the more worried we became. Petrov said he had only closed his eyes for a few seconds. But he had noticed that Moll got anxious each time the guard came by, in spite of their practiced use of disguise. And then he was suddenly gone. Was he planning to flee? No one could get out of the closely guarded gully. But that evening, we were sent home fully two hours late. Assembled in front of the works office, where the little railway stopped, we were counted over and over again. The jackboots were frantic. A dozen of them went searching with dogs. They told us that if they didn't find the runaway, we'd spend all night outdoors. Then they came back, with Tadeusz in their midst. He had been asleep, nothing

more. Had lain down in the cement hut and covered himself up
with empty sacks, so that no one could see him. He was coated
with cement dust from head to foot, his rosy face, after a long and
restorative sleep, shone through a layer of gray powder. But the
dogs had already marked him with their teeth and claws, his clothes
were ripped, and his hands were dripping blood. He looked round
in glassy-eyed astonishment, still half-asleep. Did he understand the
seriousness of the situation? Not to be present for roll-call meant
attempted flight as far as the SS were concerned. Flight was pun-
ishable by death. And indeed, a moment later, Tadeusz Moll was led
down the steps, his hands cuffed, his expression already that of
a lost man. The delinquents were no longer with us. Not yet
there, but not here either. What's the name of that strange land on
the edge?

At night, as Petrov and I lay under our blanket, without Tadeusz,
we could still see the scene. "Strip!" the duty officer had ordered.
Tadeusz took off his clothes in front of the assembled work detach-
ment. "Faster," ordered the officer. Out of regard for his comrades,
Tadeusz moved faster. The officer—a strongly built, good-looking
man in a smart uniform, holding a little bamboo cane in his
hand—rolled complacently back and forth, heel and toe, heel and
toe, in his big boots. He might be a schoolmaster in civilian life, or
a post office employee. A cheery disposition, rosy complexion,
wide jaw, white teeth. He didn't snap, didn't let himself get carried
away, unlike some of his inferiors. Nice and easy was his watch-
word. When Tadeusz had taken off his shirt, his cement sack
appeared. (Almost all of us wore cement sacks next to our skin, a
cement sack gave you warmth and moral fiber.) The officer picked
the cement sack to shreds with his little cane. The young sentries
laughed: what a card! Then Moll was allowed to pick up his jacket
and pants again. The officer gave him a prod with his cane and so

directed him stylishly to the pole. A jackboot stood ready to tie Tadeusz to the stage, but the officer smilingly told him not to bother. It really wasn't necessary here. There was no point in running away. After ten paces he'd be downed by a burst of machine-gun bullets. (Two watchtowers stood over the place.) The officer gave a signal to the musicians standing up on the stage: "A waltz, gentlemen, if you please," he cried out jovially. Mechanically the musicians started to play. Night all around, searchlight beams passing over the forest, the barbed wire, the footpaths between the bunkers. "Wiener Blut," played the band. Our breath is frozen. "Dismissed!" calls the officer in a bright, sonorous tenor, and the troop of half-dead men returns to the camp.

A restless night. Petrov groans with fever, sometimes he talks to himself out loud. As far as I can understand, he's talking to Tadeusz Moll. Once, he grabs hold of me and seems to mistake me for Tadeusz. I call out to him: "Petrov!" Gradually his eyes become sighted. Then he rolls onto his back, breathing heavily. I too cannot stop thinking of Moll. Between waking and dreaming, I have visions of Tadeusz Moll at the stake.

In the morning at roll-call and as we march out, we are astonished to see him standing there just the same as last night. So it is possible to survive a night hungry, freezing, without sleep. Only now did I notice that just one of the men was actually secured to his stake, the first of them, a French partisan by the name of Nicolas. The rest (there were five in all by now) merely had their hands tied behind their backs. How long could they stand it? Nicolas had been standing under the bandstand now for four days and four nights. The young men stood in the snow erect and seemingly unbroken. Why didn't they charge at the wire? A bullet would bring release. Maybe the fact that they weren't made fast to the poles constituted a certain challenge, even a humanitarian impulse, on the part of the executioners: Go and run at the wire. In five seconds it'll all be over.

But if one of them did that . . . Would the others then not have to suffer for even longer? And Nicolas was tied, he couldn't get away. So perhaps that last humanitarian impulse was actually nothing but a last fiendish provocation. Oh yes, that was something they shone at, such refinements of physical and mental torture.

Why didn't they run away, Tadeusz and his new mates? Was it a form of desperate solidarity, or was it another inhibition of a sort hard to gauge? Did they want to die in full consciousness of their martyrdom? Why did a man insist on draining the cup of his life to the last drop, even if it was only humiliation and torment? Or did it have something else to offer after all? Did it have some value of which the rest of us were not aware? I have thought about these questions a long time. There is no answer. No one standing beneath those gallows was able to leave report, not so much as a word.

But perhaps there is an answer after all. A fictional answer: Do the men under the gallows think? Of course they think. Do they talk to one another? Perhaps at night. What do they say? What goes through their minds? What do they see with their eyes? One thing one mustn't forget: hunger and exhaustion have certainly diminished their ability to think and feel. But perhaps life, compressed into that tiny remaining time, sharpened by barely imaginable sufferings, perhaps life has become distilled to some quintessence of itself . . . No, we won't presume that the hours spent standing under the gallows raise one's consciousness of existence. That would be water on the mills of the despisers of life. Let's take it at face value: dying means dying.

"Listen," the first delinquent, Nicolas, could have said to Tadeusz Moll, "don't stand there so still, otherwise you'll freeze. Move. Shift your weight about continuously, that helps. From one leg to the other. Tense your muscles, then relax them, tense, relax . . ."

Tadeusz made no reply. His eyes seem to say, what's the point?

But he does it anyway. He shifts his weight from one foot to the other, then from the heel to the ball of the foot and back. After a while he notices that he is feeling the most varied relief. He starts to move his whole body. A rhythm of circular motions from neck to shoulder, to his torso, to his thighs . . . A strange clarity becomes his. What a good thing to feel his muscles, to drink in the air, the cold, clean air. What will happen? Does Tadeusz still believe in the possibility of rescue? No, this time is for real, he thinks, with a fleeting spasm of nausea. Didn't even Jesus tremble on the eve of his crucifixion: "O my Father, if this cup may not pass away from me, except I drink it, thy will be done . . ."

Tadeusz feels his feet turning numb. In his hands, which he can't move, he feels a thousand needle-pricks, but then his hands too go numb. It's no good, the cold is entering him. But he doesn't give up. He looks at his comrades either side of him, each lost in thought. Then Tadeusz smiles. Not from pity or sympathy with these men, or with himself. Tadeusz Moll no longer exists as such. There is only his spirit. ("When the body suffers, the soul ought to laugh!") Man lives in the universe, on this planet, in a country, in a house— in himself. The last resource is love. Whoever doesn't know love will not find anything else, not the tiniest chamber in his breast where he may warm himself. ("Why am I thinking of Jesus, am I a Christian?") He is no Christian. He doesn't believe in God, or in miracles. ("I read all those stories of massacres of Jews in England, in Spain, in Germany. Stories of wise and steadfast rabbis who with their own hands killed women and children rather than let them abandon their faith. Stories of the ending of whole communities in conflagration. But the story of the Jew Jesus—he preached love! Didn't the Hasidim also talk of love? The all-powerful and omnipresent love of God, equally present therefore for Jews and Christians and atheists!") He doesn't believe in miracles. But isn't this life a miracle, this body he will shortly quit? (He has already quit it. Tadeusz means that he has stepped outside himself and is

now contemplating everything calmly.) His blood is still circulat-
ing, his heart is beating lightly and evenly, his whole edifice is calm.
Like an ecstasy, his understanding of his body overcomes him, as
though he could slip into its capillaries and witness its continuous
creation. This body is a crystal, formed over millions of years, a
mystery and a part of the world. He feels the ground under his feet,
the curvature of the earth as if it could breathe, this heavy, warm,
extraordinary spinning mass, whose orbit he feels, this racing orbit
through space, which at the same time is rest, unrest, likeness. Substance, the connectedness of all things. He doesn't see the forest,
only shadows against a pale sky. The moon is hidden behind
clouds. Only the posts he can see, made of untreated fir, the beams
of light and the shadows of men in furs and boots, plodding sleep-
ily back and forth over the snow. He loves the fir trunks and the
beams of light, he loves the air, the cold, the lonesome moon,
because all of them together make up life. Tadeusz feels the touch
of the air as a mother's tenderness, he can feel the fir trees there in
the night forest, as if he had long invisible arms. He embraces the
trees and kisses them, in his mind he wets his lips with pure white
snow, he breathes in the scent of the needles and the dry bark, a
cloud of smoke from the barracks under the watchtower, carried
to him on a puff of wind, a breath from his comrade Nicolas, who
is staring out into the darkness as if he can see a light in it.

"Forgive me!" Tadeusz hears one of the delinquents whisper.

For a while there is silence, and then his neighbor replies, "You
shouldn't have done it. There was no point, the dogs were quicker.
Dogs have good noses."

"I'm sorry . . ."

"I shouldn't have followed you. I felt right away, this is a mistake.
It just wasn't the right moment. We could have waited."

"It's over."

"I was a fool to follow you. I trusted you."

"I hope your mother doesn't curse my name."

"It was a terrible mistake. It would have been right to stay with the others. It's always better to stay with the others."

"We are with the others, if you care to see."

"Yes."

"I'm sorry. Forgive me."

"Forgive me too. We're going to join our brothers."

Tadeusz Moll smiles when he hears that. He says to Nicolas, "I read in the work of Rabbi Loew . . . do you know who I mean?"

"No."

"Anyway," he says. "The king and the beggar are worth the same. When the king's time comes to die, he says to the beggar, 'Give me a year of your life, and I'll give you my kingdom!' "

The Frenchman laughs. Tadeusz goes on, "And in another of the old books you can read: 'The stone lives for ever, he suns himself, he bathes in crystal waters, all the splendor of the earth is his forever. Does he know? He doesn't know. But man knows, and he pays for his knowledge with his life!' "

The other laughs.

"Why do you laugh?" asks Tadeusz Moll.

"I don't read books," says Nicolas. "Take off my handcuffs, and I'll bite through the throat of that guard standing there. That's why they handcuffed me. I fight back. But you, you poor long-suffering . . ."

Tadeusz is astonished. It's a good thing you exist, thinks Tadeusz Moll. It's a good thing that many think as you do, and resist. He studies Nicolas's face. What a face! Why didn't he see faces like that earlier . . . The dawn is graying. Before long they'll be able to admire the world again.

But perhaps I'm mistaken. Tadeusz was not filled with love, did not think of Jesus Christ. Let's assume he occupied his last hours with the beauty of mathematical formulae or a philosophical conun-

drum. All that sentimental stuff is for the birds. He didn't love anyone, not anymore. All that was left was coolness, clarity, insight into
the meaninglessness of all existence or of the void from which we
come and to which we shall return. Tadeusz had a weakness for
aviation and for mathematics (I forgot to mention it). His uncle on
his mother's side, a major industrialist in France, owned a private
airplane. As a boy, Tadeusz had once gone up in his uncle's plane.
A fairy-tale landscape stretched out below them, sea-cliffs with
hundreds of thousands of nesting birds on them, that flew up and
screamed loudly when their plane flew by. He often thought of
that flight along the Atlantic coast, even now. In his imagination he
could overfly great expanses of never-before-seen country. Forests,
deserts, steppes, and jagged Arctic islands inhabited by strange birds.
He could see people, way down in the man-made canyons of a
great city. That was one of his favorite dreams. The simultaneity of
all things: Somewhere now, right now, an unknown man was walk-
ing, freezing, through burning streets. Why was he freezing, was it
from loneliness? Tadeusz saw women and girls, always on their own
and always in the midst of masses of people. There was a train
speeding through a desert landscape. Perhaps in Arizona or somewhere like that . . . There is a young man sitting in the train. He is
returning from the war. He has lost an arm. (Never mind, it's just
an arm!) And now he's worried about how he will be received.
What will his family think: Oh, another mouth to feed! But he will
work, he will be proud, and not do anything that damages his self-
esteem. Now that he has looked death in the eye and knows how
beautiful life is. Tadeusz sees children eating ice cream in some dis-
tant corner of the world, where they have no idea that now, right
now . . . That old man there, in the pasture at night. It will be in
Brazil, or Peru. An Indio, watching over his seven sheep. His sheep
are his livelihood, his and his children's. Without them, they would
starve. If someone were to steal his sheep . . . He
doesn't sleep in the hut with his wife and children. He sleeps out-

side, with his sheep! Tadeusz can dream for hours . . . ("Can't you concentrate, Tadeusz, darling, there's only two more days till your exams!" "No, mama, I can't, I'll never be a businessman." "You can be anything you like, my darling, with your golden head, you just have to want it, do it for me, do it for your mama.")

The head, the golden head, is now in the noose. I can spin it any way I like, my friend, the result will always be the same: when it's time for a man to die, that's when he discovers the magic of existence. So let's go back to our point of departure. I could tell you that one of the delinquents had taken to singing songs at night. Another had started talking about how people live on the island of Minorca or Corsica. How they sit outside the doors of their ancient stone dwellings in the evening and stare into the purple sky. The shrill of cicadas. The look of the girls, and the way they blush when their lover comes into sight. The sighing of the sea. And the popping sound made by the pipe in the mouth of a taciturn old man. The fullness, the wealth of poverty. What does a man need to be happy? Almost nothing. A bit of fresh breeze blowing round his gills.

The following evening they were hanged. In the course of the day we sensed the reception that was awaiting us back in the camp. Somewhere in the wide terrain between Ohrdruf, Crawinkel, and Arnstadt, they had nabbed two more escapees. The news traveled fast. When we marched into camp, the jackboots were all there. They hustled us to the exercise yard. We stood there for two hours in rank and file, till all the work commandos were assembled. Every execution took dozens more victims from among the onlookers, who died of exposure and fatigue. A faint snow fell from the black cloudy sky. At last the searchlights came on, and the performance could begin. The delinquents were goose-stepped across the square and came to a stop side by side under the gallows. There was one missing. He had collapsed in a heap ten feet short. Two jackboots dragged him along and hauled him upright, just like that! He was no longer conscious. I could see the faces of the others quite clearly. Tadeusz was roughly in the middle, next to the partisan. While the others kept their eyes on the ground, Moll looked over the ranks of assembled prisoners. Was he looking for us, his last friends? Or were his eyes hungrily taking in for the last time every-thing they could see? His pale features bore an expression of slight irritation, as though they had forgotten something. ("Tadeusz, my gold, don't be so distracted always. You must learn to concentrate when you talk to someone. Leave your soul-searching for later. Everything at its proper time but then completely, otherwise you'll only come to half-things in your life!")

Most of the men didn't watch, it was the hour for sleeping. It was bad enough for them to be robbed of it. They stood there with their eyes shut, their heads sunk between their shoulders, waiting for the end. Many slept on their feet. Petrov and I, however, strained to see all we could. We thought we owed it to Tadeusz to share the hour with him, to be there with him, with all we had. Moreover, to say it straight out, I didn't believe it would actually happen. Tadeusz had a guardian angel, after all. I was quite con-vinced: the guardian angel must turn up at any moment. Perhaps a jackboot would run up with new orders that would countermand the execution. Tadeusz wasn't the sort, I thought, not the sort who . . . And twice, after all, incredible chances had saved him from the gas chamber. What was the point of those other reprieves?

That's what "forest" makes me think of. Thuringian forest, your roots are nourished by their ashes! First the officer read out some statement or other, no one could understand a word of it. Then they began with the first man. Silently. Tadeusz looked up at the sky, the black sky. He licked his lips, probably it was the tiny white snowflakes he licked. His eyes were more prominent than usual, his eyes that would live a couple of seconds longer, it went through my mind. Nicolas sang a verse of the "Marseillaise," before the rope strangled him. Tadeusz was the last. He was calm. ("Tadeusz, pull yourself together, please, darling." "Mama, I can't always be thinking of how I'm supposed to sit, and how I'm supposed to behave. Please understand me, mama, there are moments when a man just lets himself go, and nothing else will do.")

Petrov slept soundly that night. The next morning he looked much fresher. His leg was on the mend, a couple of days' rest in the latrine had brought him round. He would be healthy, he would live. We hardly talked about Tadeusz any more. Only sometimes Petrov would call me Tadeusz Moll. Once, when I pointed out his error to him, he looked at me uncomprehendingly.

11

FACES

At five in the morning, the forest was glazed with frost. But by eight o'clock already the spell was over. The ice was dripping and melting away in little tinkling streams. Sparkling crystals on every branch, the air redolent of spring. Pale blue smoke rose from the huts. Ice sheets cracked, there were murmurs in every hole, stirrings in the bark, the worms came to the surface and churned up the humus, not like tanks, with caterpillar treads, but with the easy violence of a universal movement that, had it been brought to bear at a single point, could have split the whole earth in two like a ripe pumpkin.

A struggle of cellular renewal against inanition, flow against sedimentation, white phagocytes against viruses, hope against death. March 1945. Five thousand prisoners marching east. The submerged, blind, and obstinate fight in each one of us and in every cell of our bodies ("Keep going, children! *C'est la fin de la guerre!*"), that discreet struggle could have inspired someone like Goya: the improbable manifestations of an implacable life-force. But at the same time one could have said: Look at them, what a pathetic bunch. Are they still human?

Wooden clogs on our feet, which some of us threw away on the long march because they rubbed and created sores, cement sacks under our jackets against our skin, and each one of us with a hunk of bread jammed under one arm. We had picked up the bread, one kilo apiece, when we left the camp. Of course we knew that was probably all we were getting for the next four to seven days. And most ate it up immediately. The body didn't waste anything, it had the most effective way of dividing up and storing each grain and each drop of water. The men's faces were almost unrecognizable as such. Disfigured by stubble, skin eruptions, wounds, and swellings. Those faces! They had long ago lost all the fat deposits of every day, of indifference and self-satisfaction. They were etched by privation and suffering. A few eyes were still floating in a web of tiny creases, laugh lines, and you could see occasional flashes of cunning and wit. But the whole emptiness of prosperity was blown away, the smoothness of calm days, the firm cheeks of long periods of plenty. A hard process of selection had taken away the physically and mentally weaker ones. Whoever was now on the march had withstood a hundred tests. And even so, the fifty-mile march back to Buchenwald was lined with corpses that were still twitching when we looked at them.

The face of a Ukrainian peasant dragging himself along on his wounded feet. A face like a beet field, brown and leathery with deep lines and two water-blue eyes, clear, bright, and open, like the sky over a field. That face was probably never acquainted with the sleekness of idle days. Work toughened it. Not one muscle in it to flatter or deceive, but the whole thing somehow wily and cunning. (As Tolstoy said, they feign stupidity, that's their strength.) But right now there was only fear expressed in that face, it burned with the desire to live. God knows to whom it owed such a desire, it wasn't for itself. I watched the face go lame, and a powerful will break. Rest overtook the face, an uneasy rest. On the evening of the first day of the transport, when he must have long known, I can't keep this up much longer (and each of us had seen the drama many times: a man gives up, steps aside, and then the bullet), his eyes lost their color. They became white, and they looked at us from a frightening distance. His steps became halting. Over his form, which stooped lower and lower, over his face, which slackened, lay the exhaustion of release.

Everything falls away from such a face. Everything studied and habitual drops from it, like a husk. And what remains? I watched the transformation, I had previously only seen this spiritualization in the dead. A strange luster suddenly lies on the face, and you can't recognize even your own friend anymore. You've never seen so much accumulated earnestness and dignity and purpose in him. How was he able to hide it from you before? But then you realize: a man's face is thousands of years old. The few years of his own life have fallen from it, everything weak and unfulfilled. What's left behind is the face of his fathers and mothers. The expression of the vast effort to be human.

It was at dusk: the seemingly endless column of prisoners hobbling along. The peasant murmured a prayer. Not devout or transfigured, but concentrated. Then he moved to the side of the road, dropped to his knees, his face to heaven but his eyes already closed, and several times he made the sign of the cross. No one was kept waiting very long. The ennui of the jackboots on the march drove them to all kinds of pranks. I saw a young SS man, a pretty face, a milksop. He was the first to spot the old man. Nervously he tried to draw his revolver, because usually if you weren't quick about it someone else would get in ahead of you. They were all dying to shoot, they were in a race to be first. (And surely they kept score, like at billiards.) Anyway, the young man had trouble drawing his gun, the holster fastening didn't function properly. His face was a hectic red, greedy and confused, not malicious. If he'd just been malicious, that would have been easy to explain. It wasn't hate or the desire to kill, but a sort of sporty zeal, the letch of power. (I can do it, there's nothing to it, it's just like potting pigeons!) And then what he feared came to pass: another, more agile jackboot steps in. He is holding his pistol ready in his hand. Carefully he aims, then he grins, and looks at the younger fellow, smiles magnanimously, and says, "Well, come on then, get a move on!" The boy shoots, but somehow he misses. The prisoner makes the sign of the cross again. He doesn't know, isn't sure, is this death? He doesn't feel he's been hit, but something knocks him down, he falls onto his back, lies there like a felled tree. Now it's the turn of the better marksman, he takes aim and shoots the prisoner in the middle of the forehead. He no longer moves, after that. He lies spread out on the roadside.

The face of a Jew, who suddenly keeled over and lay there. His comrades turned him over. He was still alive, smiling with closed mouth. Blood trickled over his lips. His son was standing there, a lad of about twelve. Looked about him in dread. The jackboot strolled up, his weapon already cocked. Comrades helped the man to get up, but he was unable to march. They took him to a tree stump by the side of the road, there he bent over, and carefully vomited.

"Go," he said to his son, and gave him an affectionate push. He smiled. What a smile, awkward and a little guilty. The boy gripped his feet, the father squirmed in worry about his son. With one hand he stroked his head, with the other he pushed him away. Prisoners took the boy and led him away. The boy started to scream, and lash out with hands and feet. The father smiled and said brokenly, "Please, go!" Behind him stood the jackboot, like an embodiment of death. The prisoners held the boy's eyes shut, and disappeared into the crowd with the boy. The bang was barely audible.

12

JOSCHKO AND
HIS BROTHERS

In what spirits did we get to Buchenwald? Why, with joyful hearts. The others had paid, the ones who had fallen by the wayside. Why therefore should we not rejoice? The sky over us sang out, a bright March sky, a sky of spring. They drove us into the pen in front of the clothing room, we knew it and were familiar with it, it held no terrors for us. We would take off our clothes, throw away our filthy lousy rags and have a bath. Then we would be shorn, that same evening, and decked in canvas that smelled of disinfectant, sharp and acrid. Hallelujah, humanity had survived, it had survived in us, who had endured every conceivable torment, and now lay there in the dust before the clothing room, golden dust, golden life. We were vanquished and we were victorious. The dust was still warm on the evening of this first sunny day of the year. A few of us crawled around in it, exhausted from the great test. And then we smiled, prodded each other, quietly astonished: "You? And you? I almost thought, because I couldn't see you anywhere . . ." There were still friends, companions, co-conspirators. The Jews and the Christians and the politicals were all body of one body, and kind to one another: invited to partake at the banquet of life.

I saw Petrov again too. He was lying in the dust outside the clothing room, before the disinfection. He lay there, hurt and sick and miserable, but with the winner's broad smile. His leg was swollen again. The last few miles up the Ettersberg he had been unable to march. A comrade had carried him all the way up the road of blood. A kitchen worker from Kalisch, one of those damned sons of bitches, those eaters, a devil, an angel, had hoisted him onto his shoulders and carried him up the mountain. The last

miles before the end, the gates of Buchenwald almost in sight, the
sons of bitches had relented, the ones that still had strength, the ones
that had guzzled the bread of the weak. They loaded the Muselmen on their shoulders, and carried them. And now they lay there,
the rescued ones. What next? The front was very close, the air rang
and whooped with the noise of artillery barrages beyond the next
mountain. The war might be over tomorrow. Buchenwald was big.
In Buchenwald we felt sheltered. Whoever had known Crawinkel
and Ohrdruf . . .

And what happened the next day? The next day the jackboots
ringed the barracks of the quarantine area, and drove the prisoners
who had arrived the day before up to the exercise yard. For hours
we lay there in the dirt and on the cold stones. Then the loudspeaker announced, "Jews to the gates! All Jews to the gates!" The
Jews got up without hesitating. I watched them with astonishment:
surely everyone must know, everyone, everyone must know that
whoever left the camp now was lost! But the Jews left the exercise
yard and went to the gates. In a trance-like mass, they marched and
crawled and dragged themselves to the gates. If there had been a
crater, a crater full of burning, glowing lava, and if the head jackboot in the SS office, Lucifer himself—no, a pathetic, ridiculous,
little worm of a jackboot—had barked into the loudspeaker, "Jews,
throw yourselves in!" they would have done it. I have never understood it. Was I a traitor because I stayed lying where I was, in the
dirt, as my comrades got up to go? Did I abandon them? I thought
of the gallows at Crawinkel and the eyes of the partisan, his hate-
filled, resolute, majestic expression . . . As my comrades went to the
gates, I saw them for the last time. (There was only one of them I
met half a year later, a boy from Sosnowiec, who was pulled out of
a wagon—one of twenty wagons filled with dead.)

*

Shortly after, the Russians, the Czechs, the Poles, the French were called out. Who was it, what madman was trying to bring order to this chaos? I stayed with the French. We were escorted back to the quarantine area, they didn't have enough wagons and trains to evacuate the entire camp. The executioner's hand no longer knew what it was doing. The next morning, the whole thing started all over again, another attempt to press thousands into one transport. For a second time, I was able to avoid the encirclement, and on the third occasion I took refuge in the sick-barracks, where a yellow flag was hanging. The barracks was rife with spotted typhus. The nurses drove me out with a broom: "What are you doing here, trying to get sick? Look at yourself, someone in your condition won't survive!" Three or four convalescents (they had only survived the disease because they had been inoculated against it!) crawled around the barracks in the morning sun. It was still cold, bitterly cold, but they drank the sun avidly, greedily. "Go to the children's barracks," someone advised me, "they won't find you there." I took his advice, I went to the children's barracks. And what did I see there? I saw Joschko there.

As I tried to enter the barracks, a heap of children assailed me. What are you doing here, get out, they were trying to tell me. I understood next to nothing, they were talking, screaming in a barbarous mixture of Russian, Polish, Yiddish, and German. What had happened to these children? I was afraid, just as afraid as I'd been in France when wild dogs had set upon me on the road. I turned round in despair, and saw jackboots with cocked revolvers driving the prisoners out to the exercise yard. With fresh determination, I forced my way back into the children's barracks. Sodom and

Gomorrah: I saw the four-story bunks heaped with filth, scraps of discarded clothing, also dead children and two or three grown-ups lying on the planking. The dissolution of the camp had begun. The ordering hand of the illegal camp committee could no longer reach as far as the last barracks of the quarantine area. I took a body by the feet, and dragged it out beside the door, where various corpses were already lying. (There were piles of dead beside the door to each one of the barracks.) I found myself a vacant place, slumped down on it and went to sleep.

When I woke, it was night. The beams from the searchlights on the watchtowers shone in at the window. We were at the outer edge of the camp, near the stables. There were perhaps a hundred and fifty children in the barracks at the time. They were sleeping now, I could hear the sleepers dreaming and whimpering. Right of me lay an old man, quiet. He must have come in after me. On the other side, left of me, six or seven tiny filthy urchins lay pressed together. A few of them were brothers, others were cousins. The oldest of them was Joschko, the youngest Naftali, that was all I was able to learn from them. Naftali had rolled himself up like a little hedgehog and was pressed against Joschko. Even in sleep, Joschko held his arm protectively around his little brother. I woke several times, and always the same scene in front of me: they were always lying like that, on other nights as well. By day, probably not even their own mother would have been able to tell them apart.

When I lifted my head at dawn, I met Joschko's eyes. The eyes of a Buchenwald child: a dark and earnest face. The cold and tragic expression of a hunted animal. When the little one raised his head and whimpered, half asleep, his big brother hissed at him like a cat, wild, angry, and kindly all at once. He held him to himself, not lovingly, it seemed to me, but with the primal fear of a wild beast. Inquiringly, but unfeelingly, his eyes scanned me. There was a deep vertical furrow in the childish brow. I looked in vain for the softness of childhood in that regard, for prettiness and naivety. Here, experience had plowed everything under. Had these little human animals ever lived in rooms, slept in beds, known the kindness of a mother's breast? A Jewish room, the matt sheen of ancient wardrobes, the seven-branched candelabrum in the cupboard, produced for feast days, kosher dishes, white tablecloths for the *Seder*. A view out of the window onto a narrow lane, where men with red beards and sidelocks scurry past, leaning well forward as though carrying invisible loads. The wistful expression on a father's face, the tears in a mother's eyes as she said blessings, coddled the children, laughed, and sang. Perhaps Joschko's father was a cantor, I was unable to find anything out about him. Perhaps the boy remembered his voice, the sound of psalms marking his early years.

I asked him, "Where do you come from?"

He replied gruffly with another question, the only question: "Do you have bread?"

As I had to say no, and had nothing else to attract either his curiosity or his suspicion, he soon turned away from me.

Things became a little lively in the barracks. The children jumped down from their bunks and ran outside. Through the window, I could see them poking about in corners and in the yard, looking through the empty barracks, where dead bodies still lay around. They went through everything, they dug around in the pockets of the dying and the dead in search of bread. They knew the starving could often not swallow bread, as their salivary glands had failed, and carried rock-hard lumps of bread on their persons. Sometimes one such little robber returned in triumph. The others would collect water in empty tin cans, then they would light a fire and boil up the bread, putting a half-rotted beet in with it, a find worth celebrating. They hunkered down round the stove, guarding their treasure, prepared to defend it with tooth and claw.

Once a day, a handcart did the rounds, guarded by three or four members of the kitchen commando. They cleared the barracks, and threw the bread ration in at the window. Struggle and hurly-burly.

Whoever managed to grab a piece of bread had to jam it under his arm and try to get through the wall of bodies. The nails of other hungry boys would drill into his hands. Everyone who had managed to catch a piece of thrown bread had a greedy clump of boys on his tail.

Shots were heard in the upper camp. The word went around that the political prisoners were fighting it out with the SS, with weapons they had kept buried for years. Prisoners, with hand grenades and rifles? Many refused to believe it; they no longer believed in rescue, no longer believed in struggle. One morning we heard the clatter of horses' hooves. When we looked in the direction of the stables, we saw: they were leading the horses hurriedly away. The jackboots were leaving.

All the children lay on their bunks. The loudspeaker relayed instructions to stay in barracks. Bullets whistled over the roofs. Armed formations of prisoners marched past. That afternoon we heard loud yelling and shouting from the wide treeless expanse outside the camp. A few fearless people ran down through the vegetable gardens, waving white handkerchiefs. On the road at the bottom of the valley were American tanks. They rolled, stopped, and fired, did it again and again. It was the hour of liberation. (We didn't yet believe it, days would pass before we would believe that we had been rescued.) The children didn't know what was happening. The three or four grown-ups like myself who had found asylum in the children's barracks were too weak and skeptical. No one then could grasp that the war was over where we were concerned, that the Nazis had been beaten, the SS had fled or been captured by the politicals, and that we were free. The children listened indifferently to the shooting, the rolling of the tanks, the shouts and commands of the newly created units, the calls of a few inmates running from barracks to barracks, giving the news of victory. The children had heard plenty and believed none of it. Their reality was the camp.

Only when one or two of the older boys came in and emptied their pockets of potatoes (they had opened a supply down in the vegetable allotment), a few realized that something out of the ordinary had happened. Suddenly a fistfight erupted. Joschko and his brothers hurled themselves upon the potatoes. The older boys laughed and swore: why didn't they just go down to the allotment themselves and fill their pockets, the stores are ours and the jackboots have all gone! They beat up a couple of the little boys. Joschko and the others stopped, but didn't understand. The next moment, battle was joined even more ferociously. Deadly determined, they wanted their share of the spoils. A couple of hands full of potatoes had turned their heads, just as a mirage in the desert will drive a thirsty man demented. There was a wild fight, with bloody hands and noses, and wailing. A few boys with frightened eyes looked down from the bunks, too weak to get up; for them freedom had come too late. After the fight, Joschko and his brothers lay down exhausted next to me on the bare boards. Naftali was sobbing quietly, and Joschko pressed him close, holding his head up, still breathing hard and with frowning eyes watching the goings-on in the barracks. The older boys were roasting the potatoes on the top of the stove, a delicious smell was spreading . . .

What had happened? It was the zero point of the Thousand Year Reich. The walls of Jericho had fallen, but Joschko and his brothers had failed to hear the trumpets. They didn't see the open gateway to freedom, because they didn't know what freedom was. Joschko's expression mirrored the cunning of a fox, the coolness of a cat, the deadly earnest of a wolf. I was delighted by the sight. I was in a kind of ecstasy, I alone seemed to know what this hour was worth. But it wasn't the muffled sounds of jubilation from the upper camp, not the clacking of spent bullets from rifles held in prisoners' hands, not the dull whine of Allied air squadrons overhead, battle sounds of tanks, their trumpeting like a herd of wild elephants on the paved road down in the valley, none of that was the cause of my jubilation . . . It was the faces of Joschko and his brothers. Those ignorant, frantically unaware faces, avid for food and life, now sporting a few cuts and bruises. Everything was enclosed and preserved in their ignorance: all the knowledge and experience of the world. Some might say the camp and its bestial conditions had destroyed their human substance. It's not what happened. Already at the age of ten, Joschko was a father and a tribal elder. The way he tended his little brother, never letting him out of his sight, the deadly earnest of his concern for the little manchild, his grim determination to get him through—does that not express all the greatness and dignity of the human species? Joschko listened to what was going on in the barracks. When the older boys had finished their meal and dispersed, he dragged his brothers and little Naftali to the stove. He had won the battle: out of his pocket he pulled a couple of large potatoes, cut them carefully into rounds, and laid them out on the hot stovetop. Watching them as they sat round the iron stove, huddled close, dirty, scrawny, bruised, the way they turned the crackling and steaming potato slices, and looked around them, distrustfully eyeing the hostile world about them, at the same time trying not to arouse the attention of the others, and then divided up the miserable fruits of victory in tiny portions, as if it were a ritual feast, delicious steaming food; the way they greedily shoved the burning hot potato pieces into their mouths; the patient way Joschko fed his brother Naftali, who was so tired he wanted to go straight to sleep; the way he kept him up, pushed life, hot, steaming life between his teeth, and the way their eyes shone and sparkled with their huge tiny happiness—I knew right then: everything will start over, nothing has been lost.

I lay in the children's barracks in Buchenwald on April 11, 1945, and I no longer suffered as I watched Joschko and his brothers eat. And the ecstasy that shook me was not that of Ezekiel who sees the heavenly hosts, the chariot of fire and the angels; it was the onset of the spotted typhus which, a couple of days later, was to completely befuddle me. I was lying between a dead old man, peaceably turning his beard up to heaven, and a rabble of little Jewish boys, at the zero point of the world. It seemed to me as though this sick world in its last dying spasm had spat out a mouthful of children. In my delirium (I felt I was floating, disembodied, like a cloud) I looked now at the children, now at the old man next to me, and I was astounded. I was astounded by the bounty of nature: a beautiful old man, unknown, nameless, a wise man with even features and a splendid white beard and a mighty beak of a nose that might have been carved out of ivory. He lay there on his back, not like a corpse, but a statue (his eyes and mouth were shut fast), the embodiment of human perfection: grown old, life lived to fruition and set down without a complaint or a superfluous word. When had he arrived? Who had brought him in here, to the children's barracks? He smiled in death, as though in answer to my question. He was the only dead man in all those years whom I saw smiling. He had handed himself on. Joschko and his brothers, who did not realize it, had picked up the staff he had thrown down, picked it up and carried it on among themselves. (They had, incidentally, gone through his pockets and found a lump of hard bread in them; also they had gone through my pockets while I was asleep, they found my tin spoon, whose handle I had sharpened to a knife, they used it before my eyes with sublime indifference.)

Again and again I turned toward my sleeping neighbor to gaze at him. He had not lived to experience liberation. But he had known, he had known . . . I saw that in his features. Everything suddenly had meaning and splendor and festive appearance. I was not lying louse-ridden and half-starved on stinking boards, no, I had the sense of being bedded on roses and magnolias. Joschko and his brothers huddled peacefully next to me cross-legged, beautiful to look at and majestic, and were watching over Naftali's sleep. Naftali was talking in his sleep, and dreaming. It was a lovely dream. Someone had brought hot water in a battered tin can. Each of them took a sip. Joschko gently brushed the little one's face with his hand, that tiny, wrinkled, filthy, sorrowful face. Then with his spoon—with my spoon—he dribbled a few drops onto the mouth of the sleeping boy.

TRANSLATOR'S AFTERWORD

Fred Wander called his recollections *Das gute Leben*,* "The Good Life"—good not in either of its narrow senses of virtuous or epicurean, but rich, full, kindly, generous. Its alternate title is *Von der Fröhlichkeit im Schrecken*—something like "remaining cheerful in the midst of horror." He was born in Vienna in 1917, and died there almost ninety years later, in 2006. The horror was, if one may so put it, in the midst of the cheerfulness. Between 1939 and 1945, he was an inmate of twenty different Nazi camps in France, Germany, and Poland.

As *Das gute Leben* relates, he did plenty of things besides merely—merely—survive. He was born into a Jewish working-class family in Vienna; his father, an itinerant salesman, was often away, and, too much for his mother to manage, the young Fred grew up largely on the street. He left school at fourteen, kept himself by casual labor and various jobs in Austria and later in Holland and France, was a vagrant, an autodidact. He was often hungry. As he beautifully puts it, he had an *"ahasverisches Selbstverständnis"*—he was, by instinct and conviction, a wandering Jew. After 1945, he returned to Vienna, as a self-taught photographer and reporter. In 1955, he took up an invitation to study at the newly created Lit-

---

* *Das gute leben oder Von der Fröhlichkeit im Schrecken*, published in German by Wallstein Verlag in 2006.

eraturinstitut in Leipzig, in East Germany, where he lived with his second wife, Maxie Wander, and wrote books, including illustrated travel books and reportage (most notably about Corsica and the south of France, for which he felt a lifelong attachment). In 1983, following Maxie's death in 1977, he went to live in Vienna again, with a third wife, Susanne.

It won't come as a surprise to readers of *The Seventh Well* that Wander keeps a rigid sense of proportion about his life; childhood, youth, and camps are all over by about page 100 of a 400-page memoir. It is part of the man's unassumingness, but also part of his philosophy of life, and of survival too, to keep things within limits, not to grumble or curse. His cheery stoicism here reminds me of Joseph Brodsky, who ends his fortieth birthday poem, "May 24, 1980":

> What shall I say about my life? That it's long and abhors transparence.
> Broken eggs make me grieve; the omelet, though, makes me vomit.
> Yet until brown clay has been rammed down my larynx,
> only gratitude will be gushing from it.

The camps don't even come over as the very worst thing Wander was put through: his own portion of suffering always seems tolerable to him; what happens to others is always worse, the deaths of friends and comrades in the camps, but also Maxie's death from cancer in 1977, and most especially the death of their daughter, Kitty, at the age of ten, suffocated and crushed in a landslip while playing on a building site outside their house in East Berlin. *The Seventh Well* is dedicated to the memory of Kitty, and it is her loss and the sight perhaps of her body bringing to mind all the many, many dead bodies Wander saw in his youth, that stung him, twenty-three years after the end of the war, to make his heroic effort to give them back their existence and their power of speech. The first body in particular, that of the Polish boy Yossl—frozen between life and a death no one is willing to credit—is perhaps the most nearly explicit memento to Kitty.

Der siebente Brunnen was first published in East Berlin in 1971 by the Aufbau Verlag.* No doubt, publication in the Communist East at the height of the Cold War did much to stifle the book's impact in the West; far from being, as one might have hoped, immune to such things, Holocaust literature has always been exaggeratedly and dismayingly susceptible to swings of fashion and timing. Primo Levi's is only the most famous instance of such accidents of reception and translation—the silence greeting *Se questo è un uomo* on its first appearance in 1947 (prompting the author's fifteen-year silence) matched only by the clamor attending *Survival in Auschwitz* (the same book in its American form and title) in the 1960s and 1970s. In the case of Fred Wander, it was the republication of *Der siebente Brunnen* in 2005 by the Göttingen publisher Wallstein Verlag, with an afterword by Ruth Klüger, that promises to get the book some of the attention it deserves.

Wander resists the temptation—if it ever was a temptation—to be exhaustive, to say everything, even about his own experience. "Six million murdered Jews!" he writes in *Das gute Leben*. "It's not possible to say anything about so many millions of dead. But three or four individuals, it might be possible to tell a story about!" Therefore, even in his recollection, he tells highlights, he excerpts, he suggests a paradigm, like a mapmaker he represents to scale; and, in *The Seventh Well*, a novel, he fashions, and—from true ingredients—he invents. It seems to me that—the outstanding example would be Primo Levi's *The Periodic Table*—the welter of extreme and unbearable *content* demands an exceptional awareness and use

---

* Wander was a lifelong left-winger, but not a Communist; growing up in poverty, he was imbued with a desire for equality and social justice; and the Communists he met among the political prisoners in the camps impressed him with their fight, but he saw too much that was wrong with the system in East Germany and Russia—especially after 1968—for him to have any faith in it.

of *form* to master it, in Wander's case the crystalline, episodic chapters relating individual destinies, but also such essay or prose poem subjects as "Bread" or "Faces." Though it's a complicated book ranging backwards and forwards, taking in different locations and different journeys and telling many different stories (it doesn't observe the Aristotelian unities of time, place, and action), there remains something admirably pared down about it. It consists, you might say—and again, this is not Aristotelian—of a middle and an end. It is a modestly brief account of the *crisis* of his experience in captivity, but even as it begins, Wander takes it away from passivity and suffering, no, he wants to learn how to tell a story, from the master storyteller Mendel Teichmann, the first of, in effect, his many tutors—which is what they are, through to Pepe and Joschko—in *The Seventh Well*. The book has a subtle but undeniable activist streak and implication. What, in different hands, might have been a protocol of hardiness and victimization and chance becomes, amazingly, a sort of *Entwicklungsroman*, a tale of personal development and learning. (Maxim Gorky, had he written *The Seventh Well*, might have called it *My Universities*.) In his writing, Wander displays the same measure of obduracy he displayed in the camps: a persistent desire to differentiate, to absorb, to see and hear. The shutting down of curiosity, of openness, of gratitude, would have been the end, in either case. In *Das gute Leben*, Wander recalls a crucial and oft-repeated lesson: "'A man, if he is alive at all, lives by the words and pictures in his head,' I can still hear Vladimir Krumholz saying. He lies buried in Buchenwald." But the lesson is not invalidated by that; it remains true that a man dies as much from within as from external agencies.

The Seventh Well is the struggle to maintain an inner life from what Wander took from others. It is a work of absorption. If he is to exist at all, he exists with reference to, and by virtue of what he can learn. "No man is an island, sufficient unto himself," says John Donne; it might have been Wander's motto. (The books of Primo

Levi discover and follow exactly the same principle.) Even the survival of a single man is a collaborative enterprise. And his collaborators, his witting or unwitting helpers, his preceptors, they in turn continue to exist in him, even if they perished. In its serial structure, *The Seventh Well* has something of those grand old foundationist works like Dante's *Inferno* or Bunyan's *Pilgrim's Progress*. The narrator at the center meets people, falls under their sway, older, wiser, more vehement, more distinct, describes them, gives back the monologizing Dantesque tumble of their speech, and then— like Krumholz above, or like the many many dead here, Teichmann, or Pechmann, or the farmer Meir Bernstein or the singer Antonio or the nurse Karel or the child prodigy and sleepy rebel Tadeusz Moll, or the unnamed smiling bearded Jew in the children's ward at the end—they die. But it is a redeemed, memorialized, collected death, death robbed of some of its anonymity and purposelessness and brutality. The Wander character at the heart of the book identifies himself, establishes himself, you might say, *grows* by listening—to Teichmann, to Chukran, to Pepe, to Moll. Then, when he has listened enough, he speaks, telling his own story of incarceration in the camp of Rivesaltes near Perpignan in the southwest of France—the fires, the dancing, the rats, the fragrance of lavender and thyme—where he remembers first having heard the name Auschwitz. Then, once he has spoken, he learns in silence and delirium from the silent children around him, from what they *do*, from who they *are*. And at that point he begins to believe in a future again.

There is a strangely beautiful French term, *"univers concentrationnaire"*—I don't know who coined it, Primo Levi uses it—the "world of the camps," one would say in English. In *The Seventh Well*, Fred Wander evokes and describes this *univers concentrationnaire*, while all the time insisting, by memory, by faith, by listening to the accounts of others, that there is also a real world outside the camps. Granted, the camps are a law unto themselves, a

deformed closed system, but they are not finally a separate or sub-
stitute world. More a microcosm of the real world, by synecdoche,
by *pars pro toto*. In *Das gute Leben* he puts it like this:

> Basically the same rules and conditions obtained in the camps as in
> the world beyond the barbed wire—which is to say power and vio-
> lence, opportunism and corruption—only in an exaggerated, dis-
> torted form. But there is another side to this as well, which is hardly
> ever mentioned, but which seems even more crucial to me: the fact
> that you could observe—if you had eyes to see—how a few of us
> struggled to keep alive our true and actual selves, our self-respect,
> our human bearing, some vestige of our human dignity.

While at no stage blinding himself to the realities of the camps—
the cruelty, the cold, the disease, the degradation—Wander retains
an eerily sharp awareness of what one might call the persistences
and the intrusions of the greater, truer world outside: such things
as memories, talents, stories, beliefs, and hopes. There are physical
things such as prayer shawls, photographs, scraps of letters, inge-
niously made tools and shoes, but more powerful are the immate-
rial things. In the oddest, most heroic way, these most physical of
settings—Auschwitz, Buchenwald, Crawinkel—are relegated to a
shadow-world, and what really defines existence are such themselves shadowy things as words and stories. Even in his monochrome, death-bounded circumstances, where all are reduced to
wretchedness and anonymity, he registers age, class, character,
nationality, religion, and language. He becomes aware (surely for
the first time) of the many types of Jews—not types, of course, but
individuals—and in addition to the Jews, of the politicals, the gypsies, the sexually deviant. Inmates vie for airtime for their stories—
like de Groot and Chukran. The faithful are celebrating Passover in
the wash-barracks, and Wander hears Baudelaire and *Lear*, he is
taken on phantom nocturnal tours of the Louvre, he experiences

renditions of grand opera, he attends learned debates on Flaubert and Stendhal, he can smell the air in cities where he has never been. He is made acquainted with Jewish mysticism, with the arguments of Jehovah's Witnesses, and the doctrinaire patience of Communists. A grain of wheat in a piece of bread unfolds for Wander into landscape and climate, the slab of wood off which the bread is eaten—in itself, an earnest parody of something liturgical—comes to stand in for all forests everywhere, he becomes a connoisseur (like the soldiers in the trenches of the First World War) of sunrises and sunsets, he is even able to take some pleasure in the monstrous paramilitary airs and graces of some of the camp elders and the *Prominenten*. The severe and harrowing depletion, harshness, reduction, brutality—concentration, *eben*—is replenished. In Wander's account, and, one may hazard, his experience, the camp became to some extent an unreal world in which the "unrealities," or the subversive "lesser" or "inconsequential" realities, not only gave value and consolation, but helped in the determined effort to turn this world upside down, so that monochrome became color, a board (in the hands of Pechmann) became a jazz ensemble, meals and women and family were conjured out of thin air, barked orders in German were greeted with rebel songs and profanities in Spanish, where two starving prisoners put on an impromptu dumbshow sketch of a man ordering a meal in a restaurant. And the common name for all these things? If one may venture to say such a thing, the indestructibility of the human spirit.

Michael Hofmann
Hamburg, November 2006

ABOUT THE TRANSLATOR

Michael Hofmann was born in Freiburg in 1957 and moved to England at the age of four. He went to schools in Edinburgh and Winchester, and studied English at Cambridge. He now lives in London and Hamburg, and teaches part-time in the English Department of the University of Florida in Gainesville. He is the author of several books of poems and a book of criticism, *Behind the Lines*, and the translator of many modern and contemporary authors, chief among them Joseph Roth (nine titles) and Wolfgang Koeppen (three titles), but also including Kafka, Brecht, Thomas Bernhard, and Durs Grünbein. He edited the anthology *Twentieth-Century German Poetry*, published by Farrar, Straus and Giroux in 2006.

Fred Wander was born in 1917 in Vienna, the son of poor Jews from Galicia. His father, a traveling salesman, was often away, and the boy grew up on the street, and later on the road. In 1938, after the *Anschluss*, but very much on impulse, he left his mother and sister behind (never to see them again), and fled on foot to France. When the war began, he was interned as an enemy alien, escaped, and was finally handed over to the French authorities on the Swiss border. In 1942, he was put on a transport to Auschwitz at Drancy; in April 1945, he was liberated at Buchenwald. He returned to Vienna (though not much seemed to him to have improved about the Austrians' attitudes to Jews, or their complicity), and made his way as a journalist and self-taught photographer.

In 1955, he followed an invitation to Leipzig, where he took courses at the Literature Institute, and ended up staying in East Germany for the best part of thirty years. He began to publish books of reportage and travel writing, often illustrated by his own photographs. France remained a favorite subject, and Corsica in particular. In 1970, at the urging of East German writer friends (Christa Wolf among them), who had heard his stories of life in the camps, Wander published *The Seventh Well*. Following the death in 1977 of his second wife, Maxie Wander (herself the compiler of

Guten morgen, du Schöne, a celebrated book of interviews with women in East Germany), he moved from Berlin to Vienna in 1983. He wrote novels, stories, and plays. In 1996, he published his memoir, *Das gute Leben*. A second, expanded edition appeared in 2006, the year Wander died.